PRAISE FOR

THE LAST LAST-DAY-OF-SUMMER

★ "Laced with humor, the fantastical time war plays out at a dizzying pace as Giles interjects affecting realism with themes of reconciliation, family, identity, and destiny."
—*Publishers Weekly*, starred review

★ "With total mastery, Giles creates in Logan County an exuberant vortex of weirdness, where the commonplace sits cheek by jowl with the utterly fantastic, and populates it with memorable characters who more than live up to their setting. . . . Imaginative, thrill-seeking readers, this is a series to look out for."
—*Kirkus Reviews*, starred review

"Giles gives his middle school–aged African American protagonists unique style and admirable substance. . . . While the pair manages to fix time in this adventure, an underlying distress suggests readers may enjoy greater depth in upcoming visits to an already cleverly fantastical and fantastically clever universe."
—*The Bulletin*

"Lamar Giles has written an instant classic—readers won't want their time with the Legendary Alston Boys of Logan County to end."
—Gwenda Bond, author of the Lois Lane series

THE LAST LAST-DAY-OF-SUMMER

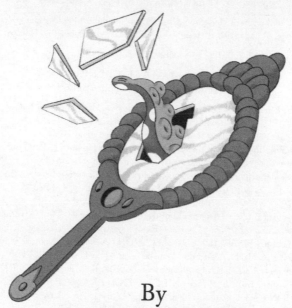

By
LAMAR GILES

Illustrations by Dapo Adeola

VERSIFY
Houghton Mifflin Harcourt
Boston   New York

hmhbooks.com

The text was set in Adobe Caslon Pro.
Cover design by Whitney Leader-Picone

The Library of Congress has cataloged the hardcover edition as follows:
Names: Giles, L. R. (Lamar R.), author.
Title: Last last-day-of-summer / by Lamar Giles.
Description: Boston ; New York : Houghton Mifflin Harcourt, [2019] | Summary: When adventurous cousins Otto and Sheed Alston accidentally extend the last day of summer by freezing time, they find the secrets between the unmoving seconds are not as much fun as they expected.
Identifiers: LCCN 2018034805
Subjects: | CYAC: Adventure and adventurers—Fiction. | Time—Fiction. | Supernatural—Fiction. | Cousins—Fiction. | African Americans—Fiction. | Science fiction. | BISAC: JUVENILE FICTION / Action & Adventure / General. | JUVENILE FICTION / Concepts / Date & Time. | JUVENILE FICTION / Family / General (see also headings under Social Issues). | JUVENILE FICTION / Social Issues / Bullying. | JUVENILE FICTION / Boys & Men. | JUVENILE FICTION / People & Places / United States / African American. | JUVENILE FICTION / People & Places / United States / General.
Classification: LCC PZ7.G39235 Las 2019 | DDC [Fic]—dc23
LC record available at https://lccn.loc.gov/2018034805

ISBN: 978-1-328-46083-7 hardcover
ISBN: 978-0-358-24441-7 paperback

Manufactured in the United States of America
4 2021
4500824880

For all the legends out there.
And their cousins.

1
BTSFOASTG

FIRST OF ALL, GRANDMA'S TEACUP-PIG calendar lied. It said the last day of summer was September 21. Everyone already knew September was a bad month with no good holiday in sight after Labor Day. Fourth of July was at least two months gone; Halloween was more than a month away.

But the real last day of summer was the last Monday in August. Cousins Otto and Sheed Alston had known this for a while, thanks to the big red circle around the last Tuesday in August. Inside that circle, equally red and in Grandma's handwriting, were the letters *BTSFOASTG!*

When they asked about it, Grandma said, "It's an acronym. It means 'back to school for Otto and Sheed, thank goodness!'"

The boys began thinking of it as an ACK!-ronym, because it meant back to alarm clocks, and homeroom, and home*work*. ACK!!

In Logan County, Virginia, summer ended when school started. Tomorrow.

And, thanks to an unfortunate headline in the latest printing of the county's newspaper, Otto was not going to take it lying down.

"Wake up!" Otto said. He finished tying his sneakers with jerky, irritated motions and stretched one leg across the gap between their beds, nudging Sheed's mattress with his toe; he'd allowed his cousin to snooze long enough, given the circumstances.

Sheed said, "Ughhh! Stop."

Otto had risen with the sun, eager and upbeat, like most mornings. As was his habit, he padded downstairs in socked feet, eased Grandma's front door open, and plucked the latest issue of the *Logan County Gazette* off the porch. There was usually some mention of him and his cousin in the folds of the daily paper, some new clipping to collect. The county folk loved reading about their local legends.

But what he saw on that morning's front page would never benefit from his admirable scrapbooking skills.

He'd stomped back upstairs, got dressed in tan cargo shorts and his favorite T-shirt. It was green with big white block letters that read STAND BACK, I'M GOING TO DEDUCE! There was work to do.

"Come on, Sheed. It's the last day."

The angry air from Sheed's nostrils puffed the sheet over his face into a tent. "I know. That's why I want to sleep."

"You only want to sleep because you haven't read this morning's newspaper."

"I don't read any morning's newspaper. What are you even talking about right now?" Sheed burrowed deeper under his covers, like a mole in dirt.

All around, on haphazardly aligned shelves the boys had fastened to the walls themselves, amidst the model cars and their made-up superhero drawings, were souvenirs from all the adventures they'd experienced throughout the season. A mason jar holding a shiny, pigeon-size husk from a Laughing Locust. A lock of banshee hair that sang them to sleep whenever the moon was full. And many more things unique to—or drawn to—the strange county in which they lived. Of all the trophies, it was the two Keys to the City awarded to them by the mayor of Fry that filled Otto with the most pride. Until today.

He smacked Sheed's shoulder with the rolled-up newspaper, then peeled back his blanket. "You don't really want to waste time sleeping on our last day of summer—our last chance to have one more adventure before you-know-what starts." Otto refused to say the S-word. "Do you?"

"Yes!" Sheed covered his head with a pillow.

Otto yanked the cord that zipped their blinds to the top of the window frame, flooding the room with bright sunshine. Sheed threw his pillow. Otto dodged it easily.

Sheed said, "Fine. I'm up. What's with you?"

Now that he had Sheed's attention, Otto unfolded the offensive newspaper for his cousin to see. Sheed read it. Then groaned. Then smacked his forehead. "I can't believe you woke me up for this."

Otto turned the paper so he could reread the worst news ever, unclear why Sheed wasn't more upset. The headline read: EPIC ELLISONS RECEIVE THIRD KEY TO THE CITY!

"They broke the tie," Otto said, his gaze flicking to their meager pair of keys; they somehow seemed duller in this morning's light.

The Epic Ellisons—a.k.a. twin sisters Wiki and Leen—were the county's *other* adventurers. Some might say they were rivals. Not Otto, though. In his mind, the Ellisons were clearly the inferior duo. Otto might have to talk to Mayor Ahmed about handing those keys out willy-nilly. But in the meantime . . .

"Come on." Otto grabbed his notepad and tiny always-there pencil. "The Legendary Alston Boys never sleep late!"

"That nickname's stupid," Sheed said, not meaning it. "*This* Legendary Alston Boy does sleep late whenever his annoying cousin lets him."

"Exactly." Otto slipped on his backpack, cinching the straps tight against his shoulders. "Like I said. Never."

Sheed rounded the corner into Grandma's kitchen and found Otto shoveling a final spoonful of cereal into his mouth. He still wasn't happy being dragged out of bed so early, but had somehow managed to get dressed despite feeling all yawny and stiff. He'd put on jeans that were spotted with permanent grass stains and ripped at the knees, red high-tops, a white T-shirt, and his favorite purple Fry Flamingos basketball jersey (given to him by Fry High School basketball star #00, Quinton Sparks, after Sheed and Otto got rid of the ghost haunting the Flamingos locker room last fall). He flopped into his usual seat while combing a plastic wide-toothed pick through his (admittedly small, but growing)

Afro, fluffing it out as far as it would go. First a 'fro. One day, dreadlocks. A solid plan, if he said so himself.

"Don't pick your hair at the table," Grandma said. She faced the stove, never needing to actually see them to know they were breaking some rule or another. "Now, go on and eat."

Sheed ceased his grooming, wedged his pick tight into his thick hair, so only the handle protruded, and dug into a bowl of Frosty Loops. Otto's foot tapped the tile floor impatiently. Sheed decreased his eating speed by half, just to annoy his cousin.

When Sheed finally finished, Otto was on his feet, bouncing and fidgety. "Ready?"

"I guess."

"Hurry up, then."

The skin around Grandma's eyes crinkled as she narrowed her gaze in their direction. She said, "Boys, why you always got to be at odds? One fast, one slow. One say east, t'other say west. Stop all that foolishness." She poked the teacup-pig calendar, her finger right on *BTSFOASTG!* "That time's going to fly by before you know it, so go on and enjoy your day, and each other."

But Grandma was wrong. The time wasn't going to fly by, and they would not be enjoying the day because things were about to get stranger than usual in Logan County.

The Legendary Alston Boys just didn't know it yet.

2
Always Time for a Fan

ON TOP OF HARKNESS HILL, the best view in the county, the boys lay in the grass, Otto on his stomach with his backpack resting nearby, his tiny notebook and pencil in hand, and Sheed on his back, calling out shapes in the clouds.

"That's a hippo. For sure," Sheed said, pointing skyward.

"Focus. We need a plan," said Otto, busy reviewing the OAAO.

OTTO'S AWESOME ADVENTURE OPTIONS
1) Gravity holes
2) Frog storms
3) T. Treasure at B. Cave
4) Bottomless pit
5) Machen house RT

"I'm enjoying the day. Maybe that should be the plan."

Ignoring that nonsense, Otto tried to determine which Awesome Adventure represented the best opportunity for another Key to the City. "We can look for the Triptych Treasure in Bosch Cave."

"That sounds hard, yo. I'd rather look at the clouds."

Otto sighed heavily.

OTTO'S AWESOME ADVENTURE OPTIONS
1) Gravity holes
2) Frog storms
3) ~~F. Treasure at B. Cave~~
4) Bottomless pit
5) Machen house RT

"Fine," he said. "What about closing the reality tear in the old Machen house?"

"That sounds scary. Everyone who even steps foot in that yard disappears."

OTTO'S AWESOME ADVENTURE OPTIONS
1) Gravity holes
2) Frog storms
3) ~~F. Treasure at B. Cave~~
4) Bottomless Pit
5) ~~Machen house RT~~

Frustrated, Otto closed his notebook and pushed onto his knees, staring Sheed down. "Everything we do is hard and scary. That's why we do it."

"Now I'm confused," Sheed said, unblinking. "I thought you did it for more keys, so you can brag to Wiki Ellison."

"There can be multiple reasons. The point is we only have one day left, and we're wasting it."

"What's wrong with a day off?" Sheed's pointer finger shot toward a particular cloud in a jerky stabbing motion. "That's a sloth!"

"You're a sloth!" Otto chewed his bottom lip and stomped away.

From there on Harkness, he could see the county end to end. Big and green, with wide fields of high grass that swept back and forth with the breeze, turning the blades into gentle waves. Grandma's house was less than a mile away, a canary yellow island to the west. Beyond it was the town of Fry. Fry only had two intersections and three traffic lights (the third traffic light was a spare, acquired in a buy two, get one free sale; it got mounted in Butler Park, regulating foot traffic between the swings and slide). Also visible on the far side of Fry was the Gnarled Forest, where the ash-white trees never grew leaves, and the Eternal Creek, which had no beginning or end. Other points of interest included Sunshine Cemetery, the FISHto's, and the many other things, mundane and strange, that made up Logan

County. All of it lay before them. All of it full of *potential*. All of it just out of reach once they returned to D. Franklin Middle School tomorrow morning.

And Sheed couldn't be bothered to get his head out of the clouds.

Maybe I need a new partner, Otto thought.

"Well, hello, young men!"

Otto spun at the sound of the new voice. Sheed hinged up at his waist, shielding his eyes with one hand and squinting into the sunlight. The approaching silhouette was string-bean slim and taller than most, thanks to the stovepipe hat propped crookedly on his head. He stepped quickly, his skinny arms and legs whipping him forward with almost boneless ease. Tipping his head toward them, the hat's brim slashed a shadow across his face, dividing it diagonally, leaving a single crystal blue eye, half a nose, and a split grin visible.

"Who are you?" Sheed said, getting his feet under him.

Otto, shorter and wider than his cousin, gravitated to Sheed's side. Both of them angled slightly away from each other for a better view of their flanks, in case something dangerous tried to sneak up on them. Maneuver #24.

"I'm a fan!" The man offered his hand. "You two are the Legendary Alston Boys of Logan County, correct?"

Otto relaxed. "Yeah. We are!"

"You dispersed the Laughing Locusts before they

devoured the county crops!" he said. "You solved the Mystery of the Woman in Teal!"

Sheed stiffened. "How do you know that?"

"Doesn't everyone in Logan County know you two?"

Yes, Otto thought, proud of their reputation, *they do!*

Sheed, always a killjoy, said, "You're not from Logan County."

Otto cringed at how rude his cousin was being. To a fan!

The man remained gracious. "Oh, but I am. I've just been away for some time. " He offered his hand again. "I'm honored to meet you."

Otto, wanting to make up for Sheed's lack of manners, broke formation and shook. "Hi."

Sheed followed suit, though with less enthusiasm. "Hey. Mr. . . . ?"

"Flux! Did I accidentally overhear you're concerned about this being your last day of summer?"

Sheed said, "Not real—"

"Yes!" Otto said. "Absolutely!"

Mr. Flux said, "That just won't do. Time gets away from me, and I'm just a simple man. I can't imagine what it must be like for a couple of heroes like you. It must seem like there just aren't enough hours in the day."

"You don't *seem* simple." Sheed noticed a canvas sack slung over the man's shoulder.

Otto said, "Thank you for your concern, Mr. Flux. Indeed, we could do a lot more good for the county if we had more time."

Mr. Flux's smile grew to a width that threatened to split his head in two. "Oh! Oh my goodness! I may be able to help you, if only in a small way. With a gift."

Even though Otto liked Mr. Flux, or rather, he liked that Mr. Flux liked them—fans were awesome—he knew to be cautious when strangers offered help, either by gift or effort. As Grandma said often, nothing good is free or cheap. Otto stepped forward, polite though a little disappointed to decline the present. "No, sir. You don't have to give us anything. Our grandma says we shouldn't take stuff for doing right."

Mr. Flux paid him no mind. Stooped on one knee, his arms lost in the mouth of his bag while he searched. Finally, he sprang upright. "Here."

Balanced on the man's palm was a camera. Bulky, with a strap to hang around your neck and a slim slot along its front, it was the kind of device that seemed ancient. Like Grandma's not-flat TV with the rabbit ear antennas.

Sheed relaxed a bit. Otto fought to hide how unimpressed he was by the gift.

"I don't know if it will be much help to you," said Mr. Flux, "but a camera like this is special. It will capture the best time of your life. Doesn't that sound wonderful?"

It did, Otto agreed, but he couldn't believe the old-school camera even still worked.

Not wanting to embarrass Mr. Flux when the gift was an obvious piece of junk, he accepted the offer, grabbed the camera by its strap. "Thank you. We'll put it to good use."

"Would you?" Mr. Flux's unshadowed eye took on a puppy-dog quality. "Would you honor me by taking a picture?"

"Of you?" Otto asked.

He twisted away slightly. "No! Of Fry maybe. This view of the city is spectacular."

Hefting the camera, Otto tested the weight. Heavy, almost uncomfortably so. Somehow, that made it feel more valuable. How could he not honor the request of the man who gave it to them? "Sure. Why not?"

"Otto?" Sheed said, uncertain, but without a good solid reason. When he didn't go on, Otto shrugged and raised the camera's viewfinder to eye level.

The lens was amazing! So clear, almost clearer than looking at Fry with his own two eyes. With his index finger, he found the shutter release. "Press here?"

"Yes," Mr. Flux said, joyful, "just like that."

Otto nodded and pressed the button.

Click. There was a flash in the viewfinder. A blinding white light, visible for a second, then a motorized whir from inside the camera.

Otto lowered it, confused. Sheed was next to him in an instant, hearing it, too. A stiff plastic square—white border, black center—unspooled from the slit along the camera's front. Sheed pulled the filmy paper free. Already, the black center had lightened, familiar images of county landmarks brightening into view.

"That photo," Mr. Flux said, "will be an eternal keepsake of the day. Would you two like a similar photo of yourselves?"

Sheed stared at the photo in his hand, saw no reason to object. Otto gave the camera to Mr. Flux.

"Excellent," he said. "Squeeze in tight. I want to get all of you."

Otto beamed and twisted to his right side—his good side. He looped an arm over Sheed's shoulder, hoping his cousin didn't have his usual awkward smile. Their picture had been in the *Logan County Gazette* a bunch of times, and Sheed always looked like he was trying to suck broccoli from his teeth.

Mr. Flux raised the camera. "On three. One, two . . ."

Another flash. Not from the camera, from the sky.

A blinding, electric-blue hole ripped the very air next to Mr. Flux, and a man ejected from it feet first, as if from the end of a steep waterslide. He kicked Mr. Flux, knocking the camera free.

Before Mr. Flux recovered, the stranger scrambled to his feet, whipping his head around, startled and confused.

He was brown, like the boys, wore dark goggles cinched tight through a mane of coiled dreadlocks that whipped about as he got his bearings.

"Did it work? Is this the right day?" he said, his eyes resting on Otto, and then Sheed. For a moment, his face flickered, the confusion replaced by a slight smile. Then he glanced sideways, at the man he'd kicked over. "Flux?"

Mr. Flux began to rouse, but the stranger leapt on him, pinning him, or trying to. The pair rolled in the grass. The way they grappled, it didn't seem like the stranger would be able to hold Mr. Flux very long. His dark goggles angled in their direction, he yelled, "Take the camera and run! Whatever you do, don't take any more pictures!"

3
Problematic Itch

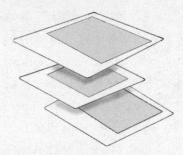

THE PORTAL THE STRANGER HAD come through blinked away, leaving undisturbed air and sky in its place. Otto and Sheed eyed the space it had occupied. They understood portals were doors, and the stranger was now on their side. So what was on the other side? Where had he come from?

Why was he attacking Mr. Flux?

The two men kept rolling; broken blades of grass clung to their clothes like green lint. The stranger drew back his left fist to punch Mr. Flux, and a silver band on his ring finger gleamed.

Otto lurched forward, intending to break up the fight, but Sheed gripped his arm hard.

"No, Otto! Look!"

Mr. Flux twisted beneath the stranger in ways a normal

person could never manage, stretching like he was made of taffy. He dodged the punch easily by bending his neck into a sideways U shape, then coiled his leg around the stranger's waist the way Sheed wrapped licorice around his pinky before eating it.

"Boys!" the stranger said, his voice strained as he fended off Mr. Flux's weirdly bendy limbs. "Get back to the house. I got this!"

Got . . . what?

At first Otto had thought Mr. Flux was the weaker man in this fight. Now he didn't think Mr. Flux was a man at all.

Otto grabbed his backpack from the grass and retrieved

the camera, looping the strap over his neck. The gift he'd been so eager to take. If Mr. Flux wasn't really a man, was his present really a camera?

Otto's feet felt rooted to the ground, so it was a good thing Sheed was there to scream directly into his face and yank him off Harkness Hill.

"Maneuver #1!"

Maneuver #1 meant run.

They got back to Grandma's house in no time, gasping and winded. Not from the run—their typical speed was sprint; they rarely got tired—but from *the weird*. What was all that about?

They rushed through the screen door, or tried to. Otto tugged the handle first, and it didn't budge. Strange. Grandma never locked this door.

Sheed said, "I told you to start doing pushups."

He grabbed the handle along with Otto. The door shimmered when they pulled together, a vibration that traveled all the way up their arms, then it opened so suddenly with an *unsticking* feel—like tearing loose a strip of silent Velcro.

Not thinking much of it, they ran inside. Neither of them kept the door from banging shut behind them, so both tensed for Grandma's inevitable "Y'all know better than to be slamming doors in my house!"

Except it didn't come.

Sheed got worried.

Otto too. He yelled, "Grandma!"

They were breathing too loud, and their pulses thumped in their ears, so Grandma's response was hard to hear. It wasn't the yelling they expected (and often deserved), but her calm, soothing voice. What they'd come to think of as the bad news voice.

"Boys, come in the kitchen and try not to panic. All right, now?"

"Grandma?" Sheed called, nervous as he turned the corner.

She stood still at the stove with her back to them like she always did when making her banging macaroni and cheese, and also-banging-but-in-a-lesser-way collard greens. Usually when she cooked, the food had the house smelling some-kind-of-good, and they'd scheme ways to get an early spoonful of banana pudding or sneak a slice of sweet potato pie. At that moment, they didn't smell a thing.

Sheed knew Grandma had "ailments," and his stomach twisted thinking she must be having a spell to be standing so stiff and talking so low. "Grandma, what's wrong? Is it your sugar?"

"No, baby. Grandma took her insulin."

"What about your blood pressure?"

"Naw, I don't believe it's that."

Neither did Otto. His stomach twisted for different reasons, taking in all the little things that just weren't right about this scene.

"Boys, I'm so glad that you two are still able to move. Thank the Lord," Grandma said, "I think the county acting up somehow. Though it ain't never done something like this before."

Sheed circled to Grandma's left, Otto to her right, until they saw her pouring broth into a soup pot. The stream of brownish liquid in her clear measuring cup was not moving, even though the cup tipped well past the point where gravity should've emptied it. Instead, it looked like something solid was connecting the measuring cup to the pot. The only time Otto ever saw liquid look like that was in —

He gulped.

It was in *pictures* of waterfalls. A snapshot where the water was frozen forever.

The flames under the pot weren't flickering; they were still, like *paintings of flames*. Sheed watched grandma's unblinking eyes and unmoving lips. He snapped his fingers in front of her face. "Grandma?"

"Don't put your hands in people faces, boy," she said. "It's rude."

He snatched his hand back. It was her voice, but her

slightly parted lips didn't move. "Grandma, why are you talking like a ventriloquist?"

The sound of the word *ventriloquist* sent an additional shiver down Otto's spine. Bad memories of their ninth adventure that summer, when they took down the Dastardly Dummy of Denos. But Sheed was right, Grandma spoke like she was throwing her voice. It appeared that was the only way she *could* speak.

Sheed asked Otto, "What's happening here?"

Otto could only think of the camera dangling from his neck. He removed his pad from his back pocket, scribbled some thoughts:

OTTO'S LEGENDARY LOG, VOLUME 19

ENTRY #34

Today was normal (as normal as days could be in Logan County) until Mr. Flux and the stranger showed up. The stranger was very clear we weren't to take any more pictures, but didn't explain WHY. Now Grandma can't move.

DEDUCTION: This can't be coincidence . . . but HOW does it all relate?

Otto said, "I have a hunch, but we should go into town to confirm."

Sheed said, "Shouldn't we do something about Grandma?"

"Something like what?" Ventriloquist Grandma said, alarmed.

They tried tipping her backwards, Otto pushing, Sheed catching. It was like trying to push down a tree. They each grabbed an arm and tried to lift her. They'd have had better luck lifting the house.

"She's really stuck," said Sheed, sweating from the strain. "Can we move anything?"

Otto thought about the way the screen door had been stuck, then unstuck when they first arrived home. "Let's find out."

He tried sliding one of the chairs from beneath the kitchen table. At first it wouldn't budge, but slowly it gave . . . like coming loose from strong glue. Otto continued the experiment. He could pick up forks, spoons, and knives easily. When he tried his Frosty Loops cereal, it was tough for a second or two, but eventually peeled away from the counter. Sheed struggled with the refrigerator door, but got it after a few good yanks. Cabinets opened fine with a little extra tug, and they could lift Grandma's biggest, heaviest pot from beneath the counter when they worked together.

They sat on the floor panting from the effort. Otto scribbled.

ENTRY #35

Small things = easy to move

Medium things = a little tougher, teamwork helps

But we couldn't move Grandma, even when we worked together. Why?

DEDUCTION: Grandma is too big to move.

He showed Sheed, and his cousin nodded. "Sounds about right."

Otto scribbled more notes, spoke to himself. "If Grandma's too big to move under the current conditions, does that mean all people are?"

"Don't call me big, boy," Grandma said.

"Sorry."

Sheed said, "You try the phone?" Then checked it himself. A little sticky, but he lifted the handset easy enough. No dial tone, though. He dropped it back into the cradle. "The camera. Mr. Flux said it was supposed to capture the best time of our lives. Are you thinking what I'm thinking?"

23

Otto stood, unable to look his cousin in the eye. "Let's go to town. Then we'll know. Once we know, we can fix it." He almost said, *Like we always do*, but couldn't muster the confidence.

Grandma said, "Please hurry, boys. I've got an itch."

4
Welcome to Fry

THE BOYS WORKED TOGETHER unsticking their bikes from the corner of Grandma's porch, and at first, the pedals and wheels wouldn't turn. They kept at it, though, balancing on the unmoving wheels, falling sideways. After a few false starts, the spokes spun, and the chains whizzed, and they began their ride into town like they did when it was time to buy new comic books, or when the mayor called them to wrangle a peeved-off jackalope.

Immediately the differences in that day's ride were noticeable. There were none of the usual sounds. No breeze rustling the poplar trees. No crickets chirping. Only the *thwump-thwump-thwump* of their bike tires rotating on frozen, unmoving gravel.

"I bet you wish we'd stayed in bed now." Sheed pumped his pedals faster.

"I kind of wish *you* had."

Gravel turned to pale gray asphalt as they came to the main road and sped past the fancy wooden WELCOME TO FRY, VIRGINIA sign. They passed the *Logan County Gazette* office, where the newspaper editor, Ms. Turner, hunched over her keyboard, index fingers in pecking position. Outside Dr. Medina's Wild Animal Hospital, Mr. Reynolds, the mailman, was frozen in midair, both knees raised like he was leaping a fence and his mouth stretched in a yell. The boys slowed.

The hospital's door was ajar. Dr. Medina hunched forward, her hands grabbing for *something*. Otto and Sheed came to a full stop, then walked their bikes closer for a better view.

"Ohhh!" both boys said.

A large python had slipped from its cage. Its triangular, speckled head angled up, jaws wide, stuck mid-hiss just inches from Mr. Reynolds's toes. So, a typical day at Dr. Medina's. The boys moved along.

Their path took them past frozen everything: cars and people and birds above, hung in permanent V-formation.

They rode on to Town Square, where they parked their bikes next to the bronze statue of Fry's founder, Fullerton French Fryer. Craning their necks, they peered up at the dusty orange bricks of city hall, to the tall clock tower that marked the time at exactly 10:04. There were a few townsfolk stuck in the square with them.

All held cell phones to their ears or extended in front of them while they tapped at some app or another. Sheed pried one from a guy who said, "Hey!"

Sheed checked it, no service—or really any functions at all, the screen was black. He returned it to the man's hand. The phone's owner said, "Thank you."

Sheed's gaze bounced from Otto to the clock, back to Otto again.

Otto sighed. Might as well get this over with. "Go ahead."

"Here's what I think." Sheed was growly and grumpy. "I think you had to go tempting whatever it is about this county that keeps us so fricking busy. You got your wish. We froze time."

"Yes, we did." Just as he'd suspected. He would not give Sheed the satisfaction of agreeing with any of those other observations, though he did note the confirmation in his pad.

ENTRY #36
We froze time.

Sheed said, "This should definitely get us another one of those stupid keys."

Given the magnitude of this event, Otto wondered if solving the problem might actually be worth two keys? No need for another tie with the Ellisons.

"What did I say after the were-bear in the Gnarled Forest?" Sheed barked. "Or when we had to walk that tightrope over that nether whirlpool?"

"I don't know, Sheed. What did you say?" Otto consulted his pad. Trying to figure what to do next.

Sheed ranted. He waved his hands in the air, stomped around their bikes, and leapt up and down in a full-on tantrum. "I said, Otto, let's just relax today. I said, Otto, there is absolutely no reason to go looking for trouble after the summer we've had. But noooooooo. *We have to take advantage of the last day, Sheed. We have to adventure some more.*"

Otto let him get it out of his system. Time was frozen, so it wasn't like he was wasting any of it.

With his cheeks puffed and fists clenched, Sheed said, "Are you listening to anything I'm saying?"

"Sure." Otto's pencil waggled.

ENTRY #37
Sheed might be upset.

"It's that picture we took, right?" Sheed said. "Give it to me. I'll tear it up right now."

Otto glanced from his notebook, having already considered that move. "Bad idea."

"How?"

Otto pulled the floppy square from his back pocket,

held it between them, explained his theory. "If the picture, or the camera, froze the county, what if messing with one of them did stuff to the county, too? What if we tore the picture, and that ripped the county in half?"

Sheed was quick to call out nonsense, but quiet when he couldn't argue. Otto was not the only one who didn't like to admit when his cousin was right. "So what do we do?"

"I think we need to capture Mr. Flux. He'll probably *know* how to fix this."

"*Of course* we need to capture Mr. Flux! Maybe that stranger, too." Sheed was still yelling, but less so. He stomped away again, shouted at the unmoving clouds, came back in a more reasonable state of mind. "You thinking a net, or a spring snare?"

"We used the spring snare to snag that chimera last month. I don't really like repeating ourselves. Makes us look less innovative than —" He stopped himself. He'd almost brought up the Epic Ellisons. That probably wouldn't go over well.

Sheed spoke through clenched teeth. "What you like doesn't matter. What's going to work?"

"Fine, I don't want to fight about it." Fighting with Sheed was so annoying. "Maybe we use both since we gotta get two of them. We'll need supplies."

"Then let's go!" Sheed mounted his bike, stood on his pedals, pumping with all his strength. Otto followed him to the next block, where Archie's Hardware store was located.

Dropping their bikes on the curb, they stepped inside the brightly lit store, where endless junky shelves were crammed with all the stuff you never knew you needed.

Mr. Archie didn't believe in neat and orderly. He placed his goods on shelves that *felt* right. One hammer might be placed with one piece of plywood and twenty nails, for boarding up a window before a storm, while another hammer might be next to a pail, in case you needed to pull nails out of something and you had no place to put them. It wasn't the most efficient system, but Mr. Archie and his daughter, Anna, were always there to help you find what you needed. When they weren't stuck.

"Mr. Archie?" Otto said.

"Hey, boys!" He was frozen halfway up his stepladder, placing a new case of mousetraps next to a ceiling fan. "I think something's wrong with my body. Can't move it."

"Yes, Mr. Archie," said Sheed. "We know. We're working on it."

"That's awesome!" It was a slightly louder, much more enthusiastic whisper from one aisle over. The boys circled around to find blond and perky Anna Archie on one knee, aiming her price gun at a stack of electrical outlets sitting next to a box of massaging showerheads. Her face happened to be angled their way, stuck in a wide friendly smile, but it would've been that way even if time weren't frozen.

"Hey, Anna!" the boys said.

"Otto, you got a camera!"

"Um, yeah. It was a gift." He was hesitant to say more than that.

"I'm a bit of a photographer myself, you know. Maybe we can compare photos sometime. I mean, when I'm mobile."

Otto simply nodded.

"Hi there, fellas." This was a third voice, more dour than the Archies', but just as familiar. Toward the back of the store, in his paint-splattered apron, holding his trusty broom, was Mr. Archie's longtime clerk, Petey.

"Hey, Petey!" said the boys.

"This another one of your adventures?" he asked through a barely parted frown. Unlike Anna, Petey always seemed a little sad.

"It is. Sorry," said Sheed, shooting a pointed look Otto's way.

Mr. Archie said, "How can we help you boys? I don't think we can actually help, since we're unable to move, but we can still point you in the right direction."

"Thank you, sir." Otto consulted his notes. "We need . . ."

As he rattled off the items on his list, Mr. Archie yelled directions that had the boys running all over, like a scavenger hunt. Big fishing nets on aisle six by the light switches. A length of rope from aisle four, right by the machine that made spare keys. Otto and Sheed bounced about, filling a cart with everything they needed to make two big ole traps.

Sheed, who was pushing the cart, skidded to a stop. "We're making human traps."

"Yeah?"

He looked over their supplies, and they were good human-trap-making supplies, but . . . "The way Mr. Flux twisted and stretched when he was fighting the stranger. That seem human to you?"

No. It did not. Otto knew what Sheed was getting at. "The human trap . . ."

"Might not work," Sheed finished.

That was a problem. Before Otto could consult his pad for a possible solution, a mighty racket sounded outside.

"What now?" Sheed asked.

Otto had no clue, and that startled him. Since time had frozen, one consistent thing he'd noted was there'd been no true noise. Now there was shouting—a bunch of it. The sound of a lot of feet, like the marching band in the annual Fry Peanut Festival parade. Only fast, and coming closer.

The boys faced the store window, watched as a bunch of strange-looking people stampeded by. Some waved their hands frantically, shouting in horror. Some looked over their shoulders instead of in front of them and ran smack into the frozen cars. They rebounded off, adjusted their course, and kept going. There were men, and women, and people who seemed the height of little kids but had flat stubby heads and wore pastel suits in various colors, so they looked like short, running sticks of chalk. Some of the odd people were in rumpled pajamas with matching floppy hats. Some were in suspenders, neckties, and . . . football pads?

One particularly creepy lady had dingy dark hair and sharp fangs, and instead of running appeared to be riding a bed of fog that zoomed around all the others like a hoverboard.

The only thing all of them seemed to have in common was fear.

Who were they? Why weren't they stuck in time like everyone else? What were they so scared of?

The sprinting crowd thinned, then passed completely. There was a moment of silence before the ground started shaking again. This tremor was more extreme, caused by something bigger than a strange stampede. Something that had frightened all those people.

Something that was coming toward the store.

"Boys," Mr. Archie said, a slight crack in his voice, "that don't sound good."

Mr. Archie's neck was turned so he could not see the window, could not see what the boys saw beyond it. Mr. Archie was lucky.

"Otto," said Sheed.

"Sheed," said Otto.

That's all they said.

The giant, furry leg dropped slowly into view, as thick as an elephant's. It extended up beyond the frame of Mr. Archie's display window, attached to some ginormous body they couldn't see, or imagine. Yet.

Whatever the creature was, it had stolen their words without much effort at all.

5
The Word Is *Platypus!*

BUSHY, COARSE HAIR FLUFFED from the maybe-a-leg. Another long *something* lowered into view. It was hairless and twitched like a puppy's nose. Warm air puffed from what must be a snout, fogging the window. The cloudy glass cleared quickly, revealing more of the thing's head, including the circular edge of an eye that was as big as a manhole cover.

"Freeze." Sheed became a mannequin posed in a bad dance move.

Fighting the urge to argue, Otto did as told and took on a stiff pose, like a robot about to go jogging. They stared bravely into the creature's eye without blinking, and it stared back.

Whatever this beast was, it seemed to ignore all the frozen things and people spread around town. If it only went after things that moved, then they'd be safe if they remained stone still. Hopefully.

Staying stone still was easier said than done.

Otto hadn't thought his freeze pose through, having put more weight on his left leg than his right, as if he was getting set to run a race. Now that left leg was growing tired and felt moments from quivering. His eyes watered from no blinking. His nose itched. The tag on his T-shirt tickled the back of his neck.

Otto focused on the creature, which was large enough to be a monster, but not really gruesome like a monster. Its eyes were a soft brown like fall leaves, its steam-puffing snout something like a duck's beak. A strange and funny word—*platypus!*—came to mind. It almost made him giggle. That would've been bad.

Sweat dampened Otto's forehead. A bead ran toward his eye.

The Platypus-Thing puffed one last gout of steam, then turned away, continuing slowly down the street in the same direction as the mysterious mob.

Sheed and Otto maintained their stances for a few moments after the creature was no longer visible. They waited until the vibrations of its lumbering footsteps ceased before daring to move. When they finally relaxed their muscles, they found themselves gasping, more exhausted by stillness than running a hundred-yard dash. Sometimes waiting was the hardest thing of all.

"What was that?" Otto knew deep down the word *platypus* wasn't exactly right.

"I don't know," said Sheed, "but we're going to need a bigger net."

6
Elephants It Is

"HEY THERE, FELLAS," MR. ARCHIE SAID. "Was that an earthquake?"

The boys exchanged glances. Neither wanted to lie to Mr. Archie, but they also didn't want to frighten him by telling him there was a big strange beast in Fry that he couldn't run away from, even if he wanted to. Otto gave Sheed an I-don't-know-what-to-do shrug. Sheed slapped his forehead, then stepped forward, mumbling, "I'll take care of it."

"Mr. Archie," he began, "it wasn't an earthquake. It was more like an elephant, but not an elephant."

"Really?"

Sheed felt terrible, thinking he'd scared Mr. Archie. But then . . .

"I *love* elephants. Don't you love elephants, Anna?"

From her aisle, Anna said, "Sure do! Especially when

they spray water from their trunks. What about you, Petey?"

"They poop real big, but other than that, they're all right," Petey said from the back of the store. "I guess."

Sheed said, "Actually—"

Otto grabbed Sheed's arm, shook his head, whispered, "I think grownups hear what they need to sometimes."

Sheed stroked his chin, considering. Then agreed. "Actually, Mr. Archie, I think we're done shopping."

"Well, that was fast! I'll just add it to the tab. When I can move again, I mean."

Since the last time they'd saved the city (those Laughing Locusts were a pretty big deal), Mayor Ahmed had opened an account in Otto's and Sheed's names for emergencies. Good thing, too. Because being legendary didn't pay well. Or at all.

"Thanks, Mr. Archie!" they said together, gathering all their goods into a couple of canvas bags they could hang from their handlebars.

"Bye, Anna," said Sheed.

"Bye, boys! Good luck."

Otto said, "See you later, Petey."

"I suppose."

With supplies in hand, the cousins stepped to the glass double doors separating them from the bright day and paused. Sheed's palms were sweaty. Otto's tummy did flip-flops. They were afraid.

Logan County was nothing if not surprising. They'd faced many scary things, but nothing like a bendy man, giant platypus, or frozen time.

Otto swallowed a lump in his throat. "Grandma says there's nothing wrong with being afraid."

"You can't be brave without fear." Sheed recited one of Grandma's many wise sayings. They thought about her words a lot when facing the strange things in their world. Now she needed their help. They would be brave for Grandma, and everyone else in Fry. It was what legends did.

They each pressed a palm against the door and pushed on.

7
Pausing the Best Part

THE LEGENDARY ALSTON BOYS' agreed-upon bravery got them as far as the sidewalk outside of Mr. Archie's Hardware. Their next course of action had seemed like a no-brainer—find and capture Mr. Flux, possibly the stranger from the portal, too. Until they saw the street.

You might expect a stampeding mob, particularly one chased by a giant, furry, duck-billed "elephant," to leave a bit of disarray in its path. An overturned trash can would not be surprising. Perhaps a toppled bench. One might understand a trampled bush or two. Indeed, all of those things were left as evidence of the event. There was more, though. So. Much. More.

"That car"—Sheed pointed a shaky finger at the vehicle several dozen yards away—"should not do that."

It was a way-back-in-the-day car that belonged to Mr.

Green, the local back-in-the-day car expert. Big and red and maybe as old as Grandma. Also, it was upside down.

Not sitting on its roof like a normal upside-down car would be, but flipped tires-to-the-sky, in midair, high enough to roll a basketball beneath it. It wasn't touching the ground at all.

Other objects were positioned in unusually impossible ways. A lamppost had been broken in half like a pretzel stick. Instead of toppling to the ground next to the base it was once connected to, it hung diagonally in the air, as if on strings. The back window of another car was shattered, but the glass shards had not fallen; they hovered like ice chunks floating in still water.

Slowly, carefully, the boys approached the scene of suspended destruction, where things that were crushed, thrown, or knocked over took their sweet time hitting the ground.

No, Otto thought, *it's not taking any time at all.*

He squinted at a chunk of broken asphalt that had sprung from a pothole in the center of the street before fixing itself in the air, as stationary as a brick set in the center of a longstanding wall.

Sheed examined other hanging debris. "It's like when we pause a movie."

"Yes!" Otto agreed in a flash of understanding. He snatched his pad from his pocket, jotted down his deduction while waiting for his cousin to catch up. "A giant monster movie. See?"

He swept an arm toward the end of the street, along the path of destruction. "The mob came from that way. All of them running into things." He pointed to tilted (not fallen) trash cans, tipped (and angled precariously) newspaper boxes, and benches, and merchant signs, and other small messes. "Then the creature came." Otto motioned to the larger objects, the lamppost, and the flipped car.

Sheed's eyes widened, getting it. "Oh! When *they*

touched this stuff, they unfroze it like we did with Grandma's forks and our bikes, but just for a second."

"Right. The moment they weren't touching it"—he motioned to that piece of asphalt hovering at chest level —"it refroze in time wherever they left it. Even if they left it in the air."

ENTRY #38

The rules are different for the mob and that creature than they are for us.

<u>We</u> can unstick little stuff, with some effort, but our stuff stays unstuck.

<u>They</u> seem to unstick stuff easy—just by running into things—but their stuff becomes stuck again right after.

Why?

DEDUCTION: Unclear. More experimentation is in order.

Sheed stepped closer, gently poked the hunk of

suspended road. There was a delay, no more than a second, and it fell to their feet with a solid *thunk*.

They leapt backwards and said, "Whoa!"

Otto knelt and picked up the chunk easily, even though it was kind of heavy. It had none of the stickiness of other frozen stuff they'd tried to move before. He scribbled furiously in his notepad. "We should try some of the other suspended items."

Before he finished the sentence, Sheed jogged over to the upside-down car. "I got you."

"Be careful." A car suddenly falling to the ground might be way more destructive—and dangerous—than a chunk of asphalt.

Sheed judged the farthest distance his long and scrawny arms could stretch and still touch the vehicle. Settled in that position, he flattened his palm against the back-in-the-day car's door.

It didn't fall, as Otto had suspected, given its size. Though something *was* happening.

"It's vibrating," Sheed said, his teeth chattering from the tremor running up his arm. "I can feel it."

"I can *see* it." The air around the car shimmered, like road heat on the hottest days.

Sheed pulled his hand from the car, and the shimmering stopped.

"Are you okay?" Otto asked.

He looked at his hand, curled and uncurled his fingers. "I'm good. My hand's a little tingly."

Otto said, "Let's both try it."

They took a deep breath together, as they always did before trying some big new thing, like creating their Legendary Maneuvers. After a silent countdown from three, they each thrust a hand forward, smacking the side of the car. There was the same vibration as before—Otto thought it felt like holding the handle of Grandma's vacuum that time he tried sucking up her curtains. Then the car unstuck and crashed to the ground with a groan of metal as its roof pancaked under its weight. The boys leapt backward, grinning.

"What do you think it means?" asked Sheed, circling the car, examining it for any other strange clues.

Otto was slow answering, returning to notes, his tiny pencil flying across the page.

ENTRY #39

PREVIOUS DEDUCTION: ~~Grandma is too big to move. (Maybe all people are?)~~

The back-in-the-day car is huge. Since me and Sheed were able to unstick it when we worked together,

> size can't be the reason we couldn't
> unstick Grandma. She's way smaller
> than a car.

Otto stopped writing. "Everything we've been able to move so far has been something not alive. Forks. Pots. The stuff we got from the hardware store."

Sheed caught on quickly, his expression grave. "That's why we couldn't move Grandma. She's a person. Not a thing."

Otto continued his notation.

> We can move stuff, but not people,
> because . . .

> DEDUCTION: People aren't things.

Sheed kept examining the flipped car. Kneeling, squinting through its broken windows, so he saw Otto's stout legs on the other side. "We really need to find Flux and that stranger fast. If we can't unstick people on our own, we'll make them do it."

"Noooooooo."

Sheed sprang to his feet, stared at Otto over the car's back tires. "Okay, genius. You don't like the plan all of a sudden, what else you got?"

Otto gazed down the street, and he was worried. "That wasn't me."

"Nooooooooo." There it was again. Not Otto, not Sheed. The low-pitched moan came from the direction the stampeding mob had taken.

There was nothing for them to argue about this time. They'd been around each other too long, knew each other too well to make another sound. They tiptoed back to their bikes, where they'd left the supplies from Mr. Archie's. Sheed opened his sack, and Otto went to work uncoiling the length of rope inside. It was time for Maneuver #16.

Corner and capture.

8
Shiny Unhappy People

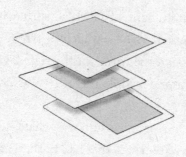

"Nooooooo."

There it was again. A sound of pain and anguish. Otto recalled a similar cry from the mailman, Mr. Reynolds, when Dr. Medina's hospital lost track of its one and only vampire bat and it bit him on the neck.

Otto worked the loose end of his rope into a lasso while Sheed carried the slack. They moved in a crouch, hunched low under the window frames of the businesses they passed. Dampino's Dry Cleaning. Knit 'n Needles Yarn Store. The Lopsided Furniture Company (Lopsided is the name of one of Fry's Founding Families; the furniture is level).

"Nooooooo."

The boys stopped. From this close, it was clear that the anguished voice—or voices—came from around the corner, beyond the newest, and possibly oddest, business in Fry. The Rorrim Mirror Emporium.

Still low and quiet, the boys crept past the mirror emporium's display window, catching glimpses of their own reflections dozens of times over in mirrors of various sizes, shapes, and mounts. Past the display window, at the corner, they paused. Otto stayed low, while Sheed stood. They peeked around the corner at the sights. One of which was ordinarily strange, while the other was *extra*ordinarily strange.

Next to the mirror emporium was what Grandma called "green space." It was an area that had bushes, and baby trees, and benches, and a neat water fountain. Grandma said it was meant to keep downtown Fry pretty, so people didn't have to look at just buildings and businesses all the time.

It wasn't a large space. Big enough for people to have a seat while eating their lunch, or toss pennies in the fountain for a wish. Also, it was big enough for Missus Nedraw, the owner of the Rorrim Mirror Emporium, to take her favorite mirrors for a walk.

That was the *ordinarily*—meaning common for Logan County/Fry—strange thing, by the way.

In the year since Missus Nedraw had opened the emporium, she'd made a daily habit of loading a bunch of mirrors into a red wagon and trucking them along the cobblestone paths of the green space. Everyone noticed it. Whispered about it. The *Logan County Gazette* even wrote a story about Missus Nedraw's weird habit. When asked about the routine, Missus Nedraw was quoted as saying, "It keeps everything calm and collected."

Not much of an explanation, but enough for the people of Fry and the rest of Logan County.

The boys were not surprised to see Missus Nedraw with her wagon full of mirrors. They weren't surprised that she was frozen mid-step, one black-and-white-striped stocking and a black clog shoe stretched ahead, not quite touching the ground. They *were* surprised by her unfrozen company.

Two people. Two *shiny* people.

Not like when you run and sweat a lot, or when you're oily from not washing your face good and Grandma tells you to go back upstairs and do it right. These two *glowed*.

Their clothes were varying shades of yellow and gold. One wore a suit with pants that looked like fresh butter, the coat like canary feathers, and a tightly knotted neckerchief the color of lemon peels. While the other wore a mustard skirt, her blouse was like a fresh egg's yolk, and a big floppy hat the shade of sunflowers complemented her gold hoop earrings. Their skin was coppery, the shade and sheen of new pennies.

They were the *extraordinarily* strange things.

They faced each other like two suns at the center of a solar system consisting entirely of hovering hand mirrors. The one in the skirt lifted a new hand mirror from Missus

Nedraw's wagon, inhaled, braced herself, and peered into the glass.

"Nooooooo." She flung the mirror aside, where it stuck in the air like a piece of fruit suspended in Jell-O.

The one in the pants also had a fresh mirror. He raised it to eye level, gasped. "Nooooo." He flung it away.

They reached toward the wagon for new mirrors.

Otto, not bothering to consult Sheed, stepped from his hiding place, holding both hands up. "Wait!"

The shiny people faced him, sprouting twin smiles. The one in the skirt said, "You can see us?"

"Yes!"

The one in the pants said, "Do we look fabulous?"

"Er, I guess."

They rushed forward, brushing aside floating mirrors that reset themselves in the air once the pair were clear of them.

"Be careful," said Missus Nedraw in the same ventriloquist style as the other frozen Fry residents. Though no one seemed to be paying her any attention.

Sheed, for his part, left his hiding place and punched Otto in the shoulder.

"Ow. What was that for?" Otto asked.

"For giving away our position without warning me."

"They aren't dangerous."

"You don't know that!"

"But we *aren't* dangerous," said the shiny man in the neckerchief.

"We're *stylists*." The woman in the skirt thrust forward a flimsy cardboard rectangle. The boys hesitated, looked at each other, then Otto took the object before Sheed could argue. It was a business card, and it said:

GOLDEN HOUR, A.M.
"Your Best Look Now"

That's *all* it said.

Otto flipped the card over. There was no phone number, email address, or website. The one in the neckerchief also offered a card. Sheed took that one. Read it. Compared it to the one in Otto's hand.

"It's the same," Sheed said.

"Not at all," said the man, "I'm P.M."

The woman said, "I'm A.M."

Otto reviewed both cards and saw the difference, as slight as it was. "Golden Hour, *A.M.*, and Golden Hour, *P.M.*"

Together, the Golden Hours said, "We make anybody look good!"

Otto said, "That's really confusing."

"Yeah," Sheed agreed.

The Golden Hours stroked their chins. The woman said, "Perhaps you have a point. Does it help if I tell you I'm the one in the skirt?"

She fluffed the garment's yellow lacy frills.

"Not really," said Sheed. "What's a Golden Hour anyway?"

"Everyone knows us," the man said, a bit agitated. "We're responsible for that special time of the day—"

"Just around sunrise and sunset—" the woman interjected.

"When the light is perfect for taking your most gorgeous photos."

Otto said, "Does A.M. stand for Ante Meridiem? And P.M. for Post Meridiem? Like a clock?"

"Absolutely not!" scoffed the woman, "One means 'Amazingly Magnificent,' and the other 'Positively Marvelous'"

"Wellll," the man said, stretching the word. "That's only after we rebranded."

"We agreed we'd stick with the new naming convention in front of clients."

"I know we did. But since things have gone so haywire, we may need to think beyond our public image until all is sorted out."

"If we're not consistent with our brand, how can we expect the interdimensional community to—"

Sheed interrupted their bickering. "So Otto was right. Like a clock?"

Reluctantly, they nodded.

Sheed bit the inside of his cheek, really thinking it over. He motioned to himself, then Otto, "I'm Rasheed, and he's Octavius. But people call us Sheed and Otto because it's just easier. What if we gave you two easier names? Is it okay if we call you A.M. and P.M.?"

He waited so they could think it over. Grandma said it was respectful to call people what they wanted to be called, and nothing else.

The Golden Hours turned away, whispered back and forth, came to a decision. "Those names are perfectly fine with us."

"Sweet," Otto said. "A.M., P.M., can you tell us what's going on around here?"

P.M. fiddled with his neckerchief. "We don't really know."

Sheed waved toward the path of the destruction on the street behind them. "Do you know what the big, fuzzy duck monster was?"

A.M.'s skirt swished from a fearful shudder. "Oh, that was a Time Suck." As if that was all the explanation required.

"What the heck's a Time Suck?"

"Extremely dangerous creatures," said P.M., his complexion dimming. "If they catch you, they just want to play and wrestle and sometimes step on you then drag your flattened body around like a rag doll so you can't get anything done. Very inconvenient. Oh"—his eyes widened, aimed at Otto—"is that a camera?"

Otto had forgotten about the camera dangling from his neck. Had grown comfortable with the weight of the device that had messed up the town. That bothered him, but not as much as these quirky strangers noticing it. He took a step back.

A.M. stepped closer. "Let's take some pictures. We can make you look *amazing*."

"No!" Sheed said, using his angry outdoor voice. "We're not taking pictures. Tell us why you're not frozen like everyone else in town."

Frozen Missus Nedraw said, "That's a very good question."

A.M. and P.M. huffed, as if the question were silly.

A.M. said, "Weren't we clear? We are Clock Watchers."

"Agents of time," said P.M.

"And as of some point today, something put us out of a job."

Embarrassed heat prickled Otto's cheeks and forehead. Sheed stared down at the camera.

Something?

More like someone.

9

nedraW nosirP ehT

OTTO COULD NOT FACE THE Golden Hours without feeling guilty. So he focused on the dozen or so hand mirrors levitating just beyond A.M. and P.M. Desperately wanting to change the subject, he said, "Why were you screaming at those mirrors?"

The beaming smiles on their faces thinned into straight lines. "Because," A.M. said, "they are so unflattering."

Sheed stepped past them, grabbed the handle of the closest mirror. It was small enough that it unstuck immediately.

"Please be careful with the mirrors," Missus Nedraw pleaded.

Sheed twisted and turned the mirror, stuck out his tongue, picked his 'fro. He thought he looked fine. "I don't get it."

He turned the mirror around so A.M. and P.M. could see the glass.

"Nooooo," they shouted.

Their sudden scream startled Sheed, and he dropped the hand mirror. It smacked the ground face-down, a small thunder crack. Missus Nedraw wheezed.

"Seven years bad luck," Otto said.

"Oh boy." Missus Nedraw's voice trembled. "It's quite a bit worse than that."

No one really paid attention to Missus Nedraw because the Golden Hours were making so much noise with their whimpering and despair. Otto followed Sheed's example and grabbed another hand mirror from the air, positioning it so he could see what A.M. and P.M. saw.

"Nooooo," they screamed.

Otto said, "There's really nothing wrong with how you look, you know."

Missus Nedraw said, "Boys."

A.M. refused to peek at the mirror. "This midmorning light is terrible for us. My pores."

"Boys," said Missus Nedraw.

P.M. recoiled. "You can barely detect the definition in my cheekbones."

"BOYS! EYES ON ME RIGHT NOW!"

All heads turned.

"Don't make any sudden movements. Very slowly, very carefully, I want one of you to pick up that mirror you dropped, then place it under the water in the fountain."

The fountain she spoke of rested in the center of the green space and was also frozen. Its shimmering water-spouts looked more like fancy glass sculptures than liquid. Since he and Otto could unstick small things from the time freeze, Sheed supposed he *could* put the mirror under the fountain's surface; water was just a bunch of tiny drops put together. But why?

"Is there a reason, Missus Nedraw?" he asked.

"Because water can also be a mirror. I'm sure you've looked at your reflection in a pond, or even that very foun-tain. So if you hurry, we can use the water in the fountain as a cage until . . . well, until we figure out something else."

Otto wondered if he'd misheard her. "It sounds like you said something about a cage."

"I did."

Sheed's face puckered. "Why you need a cage?"

"Because tranquilizer darts won't work on this one."

The boys didn't move. Unsure what to do or say.

She sighed. "I'm not supposed to talk about this, but I don't *sell* mirrors. I store them. For safekeeping."

"Like an antique collector?" Otto asked. Grandma watched shows about antique collectors, so he knew the importance of properly storing things like bronze spoons from the 1700s.

Missus Nedraw said, "No. More like a prison warden. Now please go collect that mirror before it gets away."

Sheed was totally confused. Missus Nedraw sounded real upset, and he wanted to help her feel better, so he looked at the spot where he'd dropped the mirror. A few tiny glittering shards of broken glass remained, though the mirror was now five feet from where it had landed. Maybe he'd kicked it aside without knowing it.

He strolled over, knelt, reached for it.

The mirror slid away from his grasp.

"What?" Sheed reached again.

The mirror flipped like a tossed coin, and where cracked glass should've been there was a fat green tentacle, tapering down to a tip the width of a carrot and whipping about. The cold, slimy thing grazed Sheed's thumb, causing him to recoil and squeal. He hated tentacles.

Unfortunately, when he leapt backwards, he collided with several of the stuck hand mirrors. At his touch they rained to the ground in quick succession of thunderous cracks. More tentacles sprouted from the shattered surfaces, like roots searching for earth. There were ten or twelve of the thick, octopus-like arms uncoiling from the ornate bronze, and silver, and gold mirror frames. They hopped about randomly for an instant before twitching with recognition of one another and arranging themselves into two even rows. They moved in rhythm, like the legs of centipede but without the actual centipede body. Just a bunch of hand mirrors resting on top of a bunch of tentacle stumps that

shuffled around the corner together, out of sight. A prison break.

"Now you've done it!" Missus Nedraw said.

Otto, Sheed, and the Golden Hours were too busy shuddering with disgust and holding each other in a group hug to do anything about the tentacle-mirror-prisoner-thingy.

"Hurry!" Missus Nedraw said. "You all need to unfreeze me right now."

"How?" said Sheed, peeling himself from his cousin's embrace.

Otto's last deduction bounced around his brain. He

and Sheed could unfreeze things, but people weren't things. "We can't unstick you, Missus Nedraw."

Missus Nedraw apparently thought different. She huffed. "Of course you can! With the help of the Shiny Brights over there."

The Golden Hours pointed at themselves. "Us?"

"You Shinys touch me at the same time as you boys," Missus Nedraw said. "The combination of their strangeness and your not-strangeness should reverse the effects of this magical nonsense."

Otto, always in need of more information, said, "How do you know that?"

"I trap monsters in mirrors! I know a lot of things! Now hop to!"

If the Legendary Alston Boys had learned anything during their many Logan County outings, it was that there was a time to think and a time to do. This was do time.

Everyone circled Missus Nedraw. The Golden Hours grabbed her shoulders, and she sagged like a puppet whose strings had been cut. When Otto and Sheed touched her too, she rocketed into the air, twisting into a somersault that propelled her clean over the boys' heads. She landed in a crouch, unfrozen and determined, then sprinted after the tentacle mirrors. The boys, their mouths gaping, watched her turn the corner faster than any Fry Flamingos basketball player.

Sheed turned to the Golden Hours. "Did you two know that would work?"

There was no response.

The Golden Hours were gone too.

10
The Highest Court in the Land

"NO WAY." SHEED LOOKED LEFT, right, and even up for
any sign of the shiny pair.

Otto did not help, too busy recording all they'd just
learned.

ENTRY #43

A.M. and P.M. claim to be "Clock
Watchers"-agents of time-whatever
that means. They appear to be
creatures of supernatural origin. Their
touch, combined with a touch from me
and/or Sheed, can unstick a person,
permanently freeing them from their
frozen state. An ability previously
unavailable to us.

DEDUCTION: We need to find them and start unfreezing more townspeople. We can use all the help we can get.

Sheed jogged off a bit, his eyes flicking down. "Otto!"

Otto continued his notations.

Sheed clapped his hands. "Otto! There's a trail."

Otto peeled his eyes from his pad and noticed two sets of glittering gold footprints tracing a path from where A.M. and P.M. once stood. Easy enough to follow.

"Get your bike!" Sheed shouted, already running for his.

Grabbing their supplies and stuffing them into Otto's backpack, they darted to where they'd laid their bikes in the street. Mounting them, they pumped the pedals, tracking the golden footprints. It was an easy trail to follow, though A.M. and P.M. must have been moving fast because the cousins saw no sign of them. They rode through familiar streets, all the way across Fry, past its many frozen residents. The general direction of the tracks seemed to be taking them to a place they knew well from so many cool football, basketball, and baseball games. Fry High School, home of the Fighting Flamingos.

Because it was the high school, it sat at the highest point in town, on top of the hill that rose up like a tent's peak. Riding the bikes up the incline was strenuous work, even for boys who ran everywhere and sometimes jumped for no reason at all. By the time they reached the school, they were both gasping mightily. Sheed most of all.

The boys couldn't figure any reason why the Golden Hours would go there. Like their middle school, the high school wouldn't open until tomorrow. If tomorrow ever came.

They dropped their bikes and gear, took a moment to catch their breath. Sheed removed the length of rope from Otto's bag and hefted it on his shoulder. "I'm so tying them up."

"Maybe we won't have to," said Otto. "A.M. and P.M. seemed nice enough."

"Before they ran away."

"If we find them and we think they're going to run again, we could maybe tackle them."

"Then tie them up."

"If that makes you happy."

The school's front doors weren't locked, or even there. They'd been pushed inward with such force that they'd come off the hinges and were simply propped against the walls of the school's main corridor. The golden sparkly tracks continued inside, but the boys didn't need them. Deep in the heart of the school, they heard a pair of familiar voices screaming, "Nooooo!"

Following the sound, the boys moved past rows of lockers until they came to an intersection of hallways. The tracks led in a direction the boys were familiar with, toward the gym where the Fighting Flamingos played all of their rivals. *A basketball court in the highest building in town was the highest court in the land*, Sheed once noted when Grandma brought them to a game. She laughed, and said he made a fine point there.

I'm going to be a Fighting Flamingo one day, Grandma. You and Otto can watch me hit a bunch of buzzer beaters.

Grandma agreed that was an even better point. Otto said Sheed would probably ride the bench, because Otto was a hater sometimes.

At the far end of the gym was a big glass trophy case, filled with plaques and medals and glossy golden cups commemorating Fry High achievements in sports and academics over the years. In front of the case, staring at the glass, were A.M. and P.M. The Golden Hours were not looking at the 1979 Chess Club trophy, but staring at their really-not-so-bad reflections, horrified.

Sheed, irritated, said, "Hey, why'd you two run off like that?"

A.M. said, "We're sorry."

P.M. said, "That was rude."

"Dang right it was," Sheed said. "We're trying to figure how to fix time, and you're the only people we've met who know anything about what's going on."

There were many questions to ask, but Otto's deductive

mind needed a single curiosity settled. "How'd you get here so fast? We were on bikes and couldn't catch you."

A.M. frowned, as if the answer should be obvious. "We already told you we're the Golden Hours. We're responsible for the best light of the day."

P.M. said, "Wrangling light requires agility and efficiency. In order to properly do our jobs, we must—"

Sheed, so excited he squealed before speaking, said. "Oh. I know this one. It's light speed. You two can move at light speed. Like a starship!"

A.M. beamed. "That is absolutely correct."

Otto was surprised by Sheed's guess (mostly because he didn't think of it first).

Sheed read Otto's face. "What? You thought you were the only one who could deduce stuff? Man, please."

Otto rolled his eyes and moved on. "You ever hear of a guy named Mr. Flux?"

A.M. and P.M. mulled it over.

A.M. said, "No. The name is not familiar."

P.M. added, "We've worked with everyone who's anyone. If he were someone to know, then we would know him."

That was disappointing. If the Golden Hours didn't have a clue, who did?

Otto said, "You're agents of time. You don't have any idea how to fix what's happened?"

"No," said P.M. "That's why we came here. For guidance."

The boys glanced around the cavernous space. Schools were places for information, and answers, and guidance, but was there supposed to be information, and answers, and guidance about *frozen time* at Fry High's empty gym?

"Have you found any?" Sheed asked, skeptical.

"No," said A.M. "We've yet to visit the library."

P.M. said, "We got distracted by—"

She faced the display case and, being greeted by her reflection, she began to scream, "Noo—"

Sheed grabbed her shoulders, gently turned her away from the cruel glass. "Let's go to the library."

The Golden Hours nodded enthusiastically and allowed Otto and Sheed to lead them.

Because the boys were middle-schoolers still, and unfamiliar with the maze-like hallways of Fry High beyond the gym, they relied on handy direction arrows mounted on the walls of each intersection. They took three rights. A left. Went up two flights of stairs. Took another right, a left, and two more rights before arriving at a set of double doors beneath a big brass LIBRARY sign.

Long before reaching the doors, they'd heard a soft rumbling that grew in volume the closer they got. Now, just mere feet from entering, they recognized it as the low roar of many voices speaking at once.

Concerned, Otto asked, "Are those your friends in there?"

A.M. and P.M. replied at the same time. "Some of them."

Sheed said, "Is this dangerous?"

"Oh no," A.M. said. "As far as we know, we're indestructible."

The boys thought that over a second. Otto pointed at himself, then Sheed. "*We're* not indestructible."

P.M. said, "You may want to be careful, then."

The Golden Hours shoved Otto and Sheed into the room.

11
Sylvester the Wise

ANY LIBRARIAN WORTH HER SALT would not approve of the activities taking place inside. There were a set of clear rules mounted on the bulletin board just beyond the entrance. The sign read:

1) Please be quiet. Silence is Golden.
2) Do not dog-ear books. No paper foldin'.
3) No food or drink. If you spill it, it gets gross, and we couldn't figure an appropriate word that rhymed with "golden" or "foldin'," so just don't do it.

After reading the last rule, Sheed said, "Now, that's disappointing. *Moldin'* was the obvious choice. They got off to such a good start."

"Sheed," Otto said, more concerned with the chaos beyond the mis-rhymed bulletin board.

The library was crammed with people, but no one the boys knew from Fry, and they knew everyone. Some were the strangers who'd stampeded past Mr. Archie's store. Otto could tell by their odd dress. In the room there were suits, pajamas, and gowns. Ties, suspenders, and belts with big buckles. Rompers, ribbons, and raincoats. Slippers, socks, and sundresses. Tank tops, tube socks, and tuxedos. So much variety as the people milled about, bumping into one another, tipping chairs that froze mid-fall once they were no longer being touched and knocking books from their shelves so they hovered in the air. Thank goodness the librarians weren't there; they would've been screaming in their frozen states.

At the center of the disturbance was a wise-and-wizardly-looking man. He wore a regal blue robe decorated with roman numerals. Otto counted quickly and recognized numerals I through XII. Standing on a table in the center of the ruckus, the man held a wide leather volume open, while raising one hand high and calling for calm.

"Please, children!" he shouted, though Otto and Sheed could barely hear him over the noise. "Settle down so we can come to answers together."

Sheed felt motion behind them. A.M. and P.M. had

sidled up very close. Their previous despairing expressions were replaced by wide, sunny grins. They were clearly happy to see this old man.

Otto asked, "Who is he?"

"That, boys," said A.M., "is Father Time."

"Settle down!" Father Time said, making no headway with the rowdy crowd. "Children, please!"

Exasperated, he signaled someone. Immediately, a woman bounded onto the table next to him. She wore high-top sneakers, soccer shin guards, a tennis skirt, a football jersey, a hockey mask tilted upward so that it rested on top of her head, leaving her face exposed, and on her eyes, swim goggles. A whistle dangled from her neck; she brought it to her lips, inhaling mightily.

Otto and Sheed, recognizing what was about to happen, jammed their fingers in their ears and braced themselves.

The woman blew into the whistle, and the shrill sound it produced nudged away everyone around her like a tiny explosion. All the people crowding the library cupped hands to their ears as the whistling stretched on far longer than the cousins expected. That lady had really good lungs.

Finally, she dropped the whistle, letting it bounce from its cord, and yelled, "Whoo! Listen up, team. We gotta come together, lean on each other, and let Coach show us the way!"

Low murmurs buzzed throughout the room, but no one disagreed.

"Who is that?" Sheed asked.

P.M. said, "That would be Game Time."

Game Time flexed her muscles. "Ohhh yeah!"

An uncomfortable looking Father Time patted Game Time on the shoulder. "Thank you, child. You can stop posing now."

"Whoo!"

Game Time cartwheeled off the table, leaving Father Time to it. "Well. I know you're all quite anxious about the circumstance we find ourselves in. As Clock Watchers, we perform functions that have, for some reason we don't understand, become unfunctionable, as time seems to have stopped."

The murmurs got louder; the Clock Watchers shared and amplified their fears.

"I know, it is frightening. We've never experienced this sort of change before. But, as you also know, we have not been left without guidance. Behold"—he raised the bound volume, the Fry High School crest clearly visible—"a Yearbook!"

Gasps in the room. Some of the Clock Watchers bowed.

With a dramatic gesture, Father Time whipped open the Yearbook to a seemingly random page. Jabbed his index finger to a place only he could see. "Ah! Yes. Prepare to receive the wisdom of page eleven, column two—Senior Quotes!"

Excitement spread, Clock Watchers awaiting solutions they so eagerly craved. Otto and Sheed exchanged confused looks. Where was this going?

Father Time said, "This, from Sylvester Juniper."

The room was electric with anticipation.

"YOLO!" Father Time said. "You only live once!"

Silence. The Clock Watchers looked left, then right, measuring the reaction of their neighbors. One of the beings at the front, a petite man among a large group of petite men said, "Sylvester the Wise has spoken!"

Cheers throughout the room, followed by group chants of "YOLO! YOLO!"

Sheed shook his head. Unbelievable. "That's enough!"

He waded into the room, and Otto followed, though he had reservations. Sheed was irritated. When he got irritated, well . . .

"I'm sorry, everyone, I don't mean to be a buzzkill, but YOLO doesn't answer anything."

Someone in the back of the room retorted, "But Sylvester the Wise says it is so."

"Fine, then," Sheed said. "Tell me how that fixes time. Anybody?"

Nobody. Not a word from anyone in the room.

Sheed focused on Father Time, "Do *you* know how YOLO fixes time?"

Father Time tugged at his sheet of a beard. "Not in and of itself. Perhaps there are more instructions in the Senior Quotes." He flipped pages. "Vanessa Taylor says, 'Keep On Keepin' On.'"

More gasps. Someone shouted, "Vanessa the Wise!"

"No!" Sheed said, stomping one foot. "Those're just things people say before they graduate from high school. I mean, some of it might be wise, but it doesn't help with *today's* problem."

Otto grabbed Sheed by the shoulder, hoping to calm him before he went totally nuclear. "What my cousin is trying to say is, you did good coming here and trying to find solutions. Maybe we can find some together."

"That's not what I'm saying."

"Stop talking, Sheed."

The agitated Clock Watchers surrounded them. The petite men at the front of the crowd were the most irritated. They all had scowls, and clenched fists, and pleated pants, and suspenders, and flat heads. There were so many of them, they were hard to count. Perhaps fifty or sixty. Though they were relatively small—the size of puppies standing on their hind legs—they took up a lot of space and couldn't seem to stop knocking into one another.

"Hi . . . fellas?" Otto said.

"Hello," all fifty or sixty tiny men said at once, startling Otto and Sheed.

"Maybe," the men began in unison, "you two just don't understand the wisdom of Sylvester and Vanessa."

Sheed shook his head. "No. It's not wisdom. It's just—"

"Or maybe," the men said, "you understand all too well. Hmmmm." And all fifty or sixty men stroked their chins, as if in deep thought.

Otto twisted toward A.M. and P.M. and whispered, "Who are they?"

P.M. whispered back, "The Second Guessers."

"They work with the Minute Men," A.M. added, pointing to the opposite side of the library where another group of fifty or sixty men in loose fitting jogging suits gathered. "Together, they handle some of the more tedious time-management tasks Clock Watchers are responsible for."

"Or maybe . . ." the Second Guessers said again.

Sheed ignored them, sliding past the tiny men, his sights set on Father Time. "Hey, you!"

"Yes?" the old man said, sheepish.

"What do you know about a guy calling himself Mr. Flux?"

Father Time glanced to Game Time, who shrugged hard enough to bounce her bulky shoulder pads to her ears.

"It is not a name I'm familiar with," Father Time said.

Otto joined Sheed and held the camera high for

examination. "What about this? Have you ever seen it before?"

Father Time shook his head. "I'm afraid not. But maybe there's something useful in the Yearbook?" He flipped to another random page. "Ah, Alan Baker says . . ."

The boys weren't paying attention, though. Stumped by the mystery of Mr. Flux and his time-freezing camera.

"Somebody has to know something about how this happened," Sheed said.

"But nobody in here does," said Otto.

"We have to find a way to fix this. That's what we do."

"I know, but I think we have to find Mr. Flux first. He could be anywhere by—"

Otto did not get to finish his thought. The building shook mightily, with enough force to unbalance several terrified Clock Watchers, toppling them.

"What is that?" Sheed asked. Instead of an answer, there was another thunderous shake, and another. Big, booming vibrations that grew closer and louder and faster.

"Get away from the door," Otto said.

"Maneuver #22!" Sheed shouted.

The boys dived under tables just as the double doors and the brick wall they were mounted to exploded inward, destroyed by the force of the giant, furry platypus beast barreling inside.

Father Time bellowed, "It's a Time Suck. Run!"

Terrified Clock Watchers scrambled.

The boys didn't need to worry any longer about finding the man who'd given them the camera.

On top of the beast, with a scraggly tuft of the creature's fur coiled around each fist, was Mr. Flux.

He'd found them.

12
Maneuver #38

THERE WERE SIDE DOORS in the library, and they became clogged with everyone attempting to squeeze through. Mr. Flux seemed unconcerned with the fleeing Clock Watchers. He was tugging the Time Suck's hair the way a cowboy tugs the reins of a horse, directing the beast toward one particular Clock Watcher. Father Time.

The bearded man became wide-eyed with fear. Tucking his sacred Yearbook into his robes, he ran first left, then right, as if he couldn't decide which frightened crowd he wanted to join.

Mr. Flux grinned, his mouth packed with too many teeth, like the Big Bad Wolf. He skulked the beast closer to Father Time.

"We have to help him," said Sheed.

Otto said, "How?"

A coiled length of rope was still looped over Sheed's

shoulder. He shrugged it off and passed one end to Otto, pointing at a support column near their hiding place. He pointed again, that time to another support column across the room.

Otto understood. Sheed wanted to use the rope to trip the beast. Acting quickly, Otto tied the rope low around the nearest support column with his best knot. Tying the other end would be more troublesome. Mr. Flux would see them. Unless.

"A.M.! P.M.!" Otto whispered.

The Golden Hours appeared at his side, almost out of thin air. Their light speed making them faster than the eye could see, which was exactly what they needed.

Sheed said, "Can you two get this rope tied around that pole way over there? Without the man on the Time Suck seeing you?"

The Golden Hours nodded. "Of course!"

Otto said, "Wait until he's moving, at the last possible second. Okay?"

"Certainly."

Mr. Flux did not rush. Being the meanie that he was, he moved slowly, getting great pleasure from Father Time's fear. The old Clock Watcher shook like a freezing chicken beneath his flapping robe.

"You thought these books were going to help you, old

man?" said Mr. Flux. "That I'd sit back and let you ruin my opportunity?"

"There is wisdom in the pages." Father Time's voice was as shaky as his body. "Why are you terrorizing us? Why are you upsetting the natural order of things?"

"Perhaps the natural order of things upset me first."

Mr. Flux dug his heels into the Time Suck's sides, spurring it forward.

Otto and Sheed said, "Now!"

A.M. and P.M. vanished, and then the rope snapped tight across the library floor, anchored to the far post, where the Golden Hours gave Otto and Sheed a thumbs-up!

Neither Mr. Flux nor the beast saw the fresh trap, and the creature's legs tangled, snagged by the line. It tipped forward, its snout dipping between its own feet until it was in an uncontrolled roll that hurled Mr. Flux across the room. While he flew, Father Time stepped out of the sliding beast's path, and it collided with the far wall, destroying it as it burst out, then down, since the library was on the school's top floor.

The beast took lots of debris with it—from single bricks to whole chunks of the building that looked like big ole puzzle pieces—before the pieces refroze, paused in midair, a brick and concrete avalanche trail locked in time all the way to the ground.

The tough Time Suck recovered from the fall quickly, though was a bit wobbly on those thick legs. Free of Mr. Flux, it proceeded to graze in a nearby field. Otto wondered if they should follow its lead and make their escape.

Mr. Flux was laid out on a toppled nonfiction shelf. His stretchy arms and legs rested limply on dislodged volumes.

Sheed yanked the knot loose from the post. "Now!"

Otto ran to undo the other end so they could bind the rubbery menace and get some answers.

Mr. Flux groaned, still stunned from impact. Other Clock Watchers peeked from under tables and behind chairs and from other hiding places. Anticipation buzzed through the room.

The cousins tugged the rope tight between them, prepared to pounce.

One, mouthed Otto.

Two, mouthed Sheed.

"Three!" shouted Mr. Flux, his eyes popping open like window shades.

The boys screamed. The Clock Watchers screamed. Mr. Flux screamed, but his scream was threaded with laughter. Bullies loved terrorizing those around them.

Mr. Flux's bent knees straightened, lifting the rest of his body to a standing position in a way no normal human could ever manage. Upright, he reached for his discarded hat, which lay at his feet. His arm bubble-gum stretched.

Once the brim was pinched between his thumb and forefinger, the arm retracted like fishing line on a reel. He placed the hat on his head, taking his time to adjust the fit. As he did, more Clock Watchers fled the room.

Otto and Sheed exchanged terrified glances, but would not run. Without saying another word they executed Maneuver #21: stand your ground. They'd worked too hard to get a lead on Mr. Flux to simply turn tail. That was not what legends did.

"Well, aren't you the brave ones?" Mr. Flux chortled.

Sheed said, "You're going to help us fix time."

"I already did. You wanted more summer. Now you have all you can ever stand."

"You tricked us," Otto said. "You're a dirty trickster."

"Now, now. All that name calling is beneath you." Mr. Flux took a step closer, almost in range for some rope wrangling. "While you're saying nasty things to me, you could be enjoying all the time you have . . . left."

"What's that supposed to mean?" said Sheed.

"Oh," said Mr. Flux, "I like you two so much, I'm thinking I don't want to ever see you change. Another picture may be in order, to preserve you just the way you are."

His hand snapped forward, like a frog's tongue snatching a passing fly, grasping for the camera still dangling from Otto's neck. His fingers folded around it like spider legs as he attempted to rip it from Otto. The canvas and leather strap around Otto's neck held strong, and Otto backpedaled while Sheed rushed forward, still gripping his length of rope.

Sheed, using the natural athleticism his gangly legs allowed, circled Mr. Flux twice, looping the rope around his calves.

"Hey! Stop that!" Mr. Flux said, distracted.

While Sheed drew his attention, Otto slipped free of Flux's grip. With his part of the rope, he ran around Mr. Flux in the opposite direction, doubling the loops around his legs. Sheed snapped his section of rope like a whip, and it lassoed Mr. Flux's left arm. Otto performed a similar move on the other side, snagging the right arm. Maneuver #38: rope wrangling.

The boys moved like a couple of dancers in a well-rehearsed routine until most of their rope wound around Mr. Flux, mummy-style. Otto wrapped his remaining length around Flux's hands and leaned back, drawing the rope tight. Sheed did the same on Mr. Flux's other side, so they both looked like contestants in a game of tug-of-war, where Mr. Flux was the bowed ribbon at the center of the rope.

"We've got you!" said Otto, triumphant and straining. "Now, if you answer our questions and help us fix time, we might let you go back where you came from."

Sheed said, "Otto, stop trash talking and let's get this rope tied to something."

Otto tugged on his rope extra hard. "We won. He's not going anywhere."

Mr. Flux, sad-faced and defeated, said, "He's right, you know."

"See?" said Otto, in his boastful Otto way.

The entangled Flux said, "I'm not going *anywhere*."

In a sudden burst of movement and strength, Mr. Flux spun on his heels. Otto and Sheed were yanked off their feet, colliding with one another. As they bounced off each other they lost their grips on the rope, and it was sucked into the Mr. Flux cyclone, which spun in such a blur he was more like wind than man.

When he slowed and settled, his limbs were free again, and the rope was thrown aside. He snatched the hat from his head, tipped it toward the boys, and bowed like a show-man thanking his audience. Ta-da!

Grinning a malicious grin, he straightened and replaced the hat atop his head. "Now, boys, for my next trick, I'm going to make two little problems disappear!"

He leapt forward, his fingers curled into claws, grasping for Otto's neck.

13
The Unluckiest Chapter

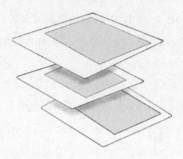

SHEED GRABBED OTTO BY THE SHOULDER and rolled him away from Mr. Flux's grasp. With some distance between him and them, the boys scrambled to their feet, on guard.

"Give me that camera!" Mr. Flux spat.

Otto and Sheed exchanged glances, a silent message, and then bolted for the door. Sheed's speed was a natural gift, one he hoped to use as a Fry Flamingo one day. Otto was less athletic, though he kept up when it mattered. Like now.

Neither boy was faster than Mr. Flux, who moved like snakes, and living taffy, and malignant rubber bands, slender and stretched. He jetted forward like an eel through water, bending his body around them and positioning his torso between them and the exit while his legs ran to catch up. His elongated body snapped back to normal human shape. "No way out, boys."

Otto looked about, this way and that, refusing to give up, because giving up was something else legends didn't do. Mr. Flux was wrong. There was a way out, it just might not be the safest, smartest route.

"Sheed, follow me." Otto ran for the hole in the wall.

There was no time to discuss this. Sheed knew that, the same way he instantly knew what Otto intended they do.

"Like a jungle gym!" Otto shouted over his shoulder, the only instruction he had time to give before leaping through the ragged hole in the wall.

They were three floors up. Airborne for a moment, Otto stretched, grabbing at a frozen brick that had been dislodged then restuck in time when the Time Suck crashed through the wall. He caught it in a good, solid, life-saving grip.

Then it unfroze.

He'd expected this, knowing he had but a second before his touch permanently unstuck the debris, so he swung to the next lower piece of frozen brick, grabbed it, then swung to the next as each previous piece thunked to the ground. Swing, grab, swing.

Like a jungle gym.

While he descended the three floors, piece by piece, in clumsy, grasping hand grips, Sheed traversed the debris, nimble as always. He leapt from brick to brick on his tiptoes, as if skipping across steppingstones (steppingstones that fell away a moment after he touched them). His pace was fast and sure, and he reached the ground before Otto, turning his last bouncing step into a somersault and landing in a superhero crouch.

Otto released his last handhold, landed beside Sheed, and said, "Showoff!"

Sheed shushed him with a hand wave.

The Time Suck that created their escape route lumbered toward them, brushing chunks of frozen brick wall aside.

This close, it was clear this particular Time Suck wasn't as large as the one that had frightened them at Mr. Archie's store. If that other one was the size of a full-grown elephant-platypus thing, this one was more like a kid elephant-platypus thing. Extra-large or not, it was still capable of doing a lot of damage. Just ask the wall hovering around them in pieces.

"Freeze again?" Sheed whispered.

No, that wouldn't work. The creature had already seen them in motion and wouldn't be fooled.

Otto said, "I think we need to move slowly."

They'd landed mere yards from where they'd laid their bikes, so it was only a matter of shuffling—slowly—to them. No problem. So long as the creature didn't eat them.

Brave, brave Sheed moved first. He did a slow lunge toward his bike, planting one foot, then sliding the other to meet it. The Time Suck angled its snout his way and took a slow step closer, too. Sheed took another step toward his bike, and the beast took another step toward him. Almost close enough to touch.

Otto began his slide, wanting to be nearer to Sheed in case this turned into a fight.

Sheed stopped moving, but the beast took a bouncy step forward and poked its snout in his face, stopping short an inch. The remaining distance it covered with a flicked tongue, mopped sloppily across Sheed's cheek.

"Ohhhhh," Sheed moaned. "Gross!" First tentacles, now this.

Otto panicked, his heart plummeting to the ground with the loose bricks he'd dragged down. He stood at an angle that only allowed sight of the beast's action, not the result. "Are you okay? Did it lick your face off?"

Sheed twisted his way, revealing an intact, yet moist, cheek. "I'm covered in giant monster spit, Otto. I'm not okay."

The beast chuffed, gusting hot breath that rippled Sheed's tiny 'fro. It angled toward Otto.

"Oh no you don't." Otto mounted his bike.

The creature did not pursue its next intended lick victim, eyeing the bike with the suspicion of a dog seeing its first cat.

Otto told it, "I ain't gonna hurt you. You ain't gonna lick me either, though."

While he laid out those simple rules for the Time Suck, Sheed gathered his bike and sponged spit off his face with his b-ball jersey. "Grandma's not going to let you keep that thing, you know."

"I wasn't thinking about keeping it," Otto lied. He was. It was cute. Clearly, it wasn't a vicious creature, for it would've attacked them by now. It had only acted out because of Mr. Flux, Otto reasoned. Mr. Flux made you do things you didn't want to do—he knew that firsthand.

Sheed said, "We should go before Flux gets down here. If he's taking the stairs, we've only got a little head start."

Mr. Flux didn't take the stairs.

A black streak ejected from the hole in the wall above their heads, dropping directly onto the Time Suck's back. He gripped handfuls of its fur and dug in his heels, riling the docile creature into a rage.

"Boys," Mr. Flux said, "shall we continue?"

14
Manure for You?

THE BOYS TWISTED THEIR HANDLEBARS away from the beast, stood on their pedals, and pumped. Sheed got off to a good start, having imagined on many occasions that his bike was a street-racing motorcycle. He'd practiced fast getaways, fantasized he was revving a powerful engine that left a skid mark and dust behind. Glancing over his shoulder, he saw Otto wobbling, having gotten off to a not-so-great start. He might crash!

Sheed slowed up, letting his shaky cousin pull alongside him, then placed a hand on Otto's shoulder, steadying him. The beast gained—Sheed could feel its breath puff at his bike—but Otto was pedaling confidently now, so his lost lead wasn't nothing but a thing. They were together. That was what mattered.

"I was fine, you know," Otto said, his backpack bouncing with every pedal pump.

"You're welcome," Sheed mumbled between short breaths.

They used every ounce of leg strength to put some distance between them and the galloping beast. It worked, too. A couple of brown boy missiles fired down the hill away from Fry High.

Otto didn't dare think on how fast they might be going. One thousand miles per hour, maybe? Two thousand? Surely they'd broken the sound barrier but were moving too fast to notice.

The gap between them and Mr. Flux was widening, as the creature he rode didn't have wheels and couldn't simply coast down the steep incline. If it had been all hill, all the way to wherever the boys were going—something they hadn't decided yet—this getaway would've been a breeze. That was not the case.

The base of the hill—a T-shaped intersection where Fry High Boulevard met Hill Valley Lane—was fast approaching. Worse, the intersection was not empty. Frozen cars occupied the road, nearly bumper to bumper, only the narrowest of gaps between them.

"Sheed!" Otto said.

"I know, I know."

If they slowed down, Flux would catch them. If they didn't hit the gaps between the cars just right, they'd wreck and become road scabs.

"You left," Sheed shouted, "me right. Split!"

Their paths wishboned, Otto aiming for the gap at the front fender of a big old frozen SUV, Sheed taking the gap at the back bumper.

"Arrrrgghhhhhhh!" the boys screamed, understanding this could be the moment when their legend ended.

Vwoosh! Vwoosh!

Otto sailed through his gap with inches to spare. A second later, so did Sheed.

"Ohhhhhh!" Otto shouted, excited, and relieved, and proud, and ecstatic and a bunch of other words!

Sheed laughed madly and screamed, "Hitting buzzer beaters can't feel better than that!"

They were so caught up in celebrating their awesomeness, they stopped pedaling. Otto squeezed his handbrake and fishtailed his back tire so he now faced the direction from which they'd come. Sheed did the same. The lumbering Time Suck had just reached the base of Fry High Boulevard, where its path was blocked by the cars. It stopped at the barricade. For the shortest second, the boys thought Flux had given up and taken the lost race like a good sportsman.

He jerked the tufts of the beast's hair, and it reacted angrily, wedging its snout beneath that massive SUV and tossing it to the side, where it froze in midair after leaving the beast's path free and clear. It galloped at them, roaring in pain.

The chase began again.

The hill had been their only advantage. Now that they were on level ground, zooming through Fry, zigging around frozen people and things, they found their bikes maintained only the narrowest lead over the creature. When they rode down the trashed street by Archie's hardware, they had to dodge all the stuck-in-midair debris. Flux and his beast ran straight through it.

When they took shortcuts down alleys and between restaurants, the beast leapt onto walls and rooftops, chasing them from impossible angles.

Zooming past one side street, Otto spotted Missus Nedraw in a wrestling match with her mirror tentacles and thought, *This is the worst last day of summer ever, for everyone.*

They hadn't been caught, though, which was good news. But good news often came with bad, and this was no exception. They were getting tired.

Otto and Sheed had the energy of all young boys. It *seemed* limitless, but wasn't. Otto's legs felt heavy, like they'd been dunked in cement, and it was hard catching his breath. Sheed winced from a sharp pain in his side, and his tummy felt like the time Grandma said he shouldn't have eaten so many shrimp.

The Time Suck was unbelievably quick. Running in galloping strides more suited for a racehorse than a furry, potbellied, face-licking thing. Flux was like a cowboy on its back, gripping fur with one hand, slapping the creature's flank with the other. The boys rode harder.

"We . . . can't," Sheed panted, "keep . . . this up."

Otto had figured that out five minutes ago, but was too winded to speak.

"We should . . . split . . . up."

Through the pain in his chest, Otto forced a "no."

If he could have formed whole sentences, he'd have explained that they watched too many scary movies to make that mistake. You never split up when the monster's after you. That's just dumb.

"Then . . . what?"

Otto swerved around a frozen cat and hopped the curb at Main Street, his brain straining in the midst of exhaustion. Maybe there was a way, something from a previous adventure. Like—

"Look!" Sheed said, pointing toward a rooftop up the street.

At the ledge, with an oddly wriggling, person-size bundle hoisted on his shoulder, was the stranger who'd dropped out of a sky portal that morning. Still in his not-from-Fry clothes, with his dreadlocks all over the place, he yelled something.

They weren't quite close enough to hear him, and the moaning beast on their tail didn't make listening easier.

The stranger cupped his hand around his mouth, shouting something that sounded like . . . *manure for you?*

Is his sack full of poop? Otto thought. *Why would we want his sack of poop?*

To Sheed it sounded like *mature coo-coo*. What?

Closer, with the stranger straining his voice, the call was clarified. He screamed, "Maneuver. Forty. Two!"

Maneuver #42?

That was . . . genius. Also, very stupid. They were out of options, though.

The winded boys didn't have to waste any more breath communicating what came next. All energy poured into the next mile in order to execute Maneuver #42. They aimed their bikes away from Main Street, away from town.

They were heading into the Gnarled Forest, toward the Eternal Creek. Which was more like a narrow river, but people in Logan didn't like to name things in a boastful way.

Not only was it like a river, it was like a *deadly* river. Easily in the top three most dangerous places in Logan County.

And Maneuver #42?

They were gonna have to jump it.

15
We Can Only Hope

THE ETERNAL CREEK WAS NOT actually eternal, because *eternal* means something goes on forever. Like at school when Leen Ellison answered questions in science class, or like when Grandma yelled at them for breaking one of her porcelain dolls.

The creek did begin and end. North of the county, it started as an offshoot from the Meherrin River. South of the county, it dropped off into a waterfall. The "eternal" problem happened along the stretch of creek between the Logan County borders.

Last spring, one of Otto and Sheed's classmates, Wallace, age eleven, fell in the creek, and was swept south by the current. Luckily he was a strong swimmer; he didn't drown. Unluckily, he fell in within the county borders. So, at the southern border, where he should've kept going until he dropped over the waterfall, he was transported *back* to the northern border and swept down the creek all over again. The second time he hit the southern border, he was transported to the northern border again. And again. And again. An eternal loop.

All in all, Wallace made twelve trips down the Eternal Creek before some folks from Fry fished him out. That was the good news. The bad news: apparently every looping trip had aged him a year.

The Wallace who came out of the creek, drenched in too-short jeans, a too-tight shirt, with shaggy unkempt hair and fingernails that were about two feet long, was twenty-three years old.

Some said it was tragic that he grew up so fast, but Wallace adjusted well. He wasn't so fun anymore—whenever Otto and Sheed saw him, all he talked about was traffic and weather—but he was the best math student at D. Franklin Middle School (to Leen Ellison's chagrin), so Mayor Ahmed let him work in the City Hall tax department and "make a pretty good living." Wallace had bought a condo. Whatever that was.

Grandma called Wallace's story a "cautionary tale."

When she said it, Sheed asked, "What's that mean?"

"It means he was one of the lucky ones, and we should all take heed. People been falling in that creek since I was a little girl. Some of them never got pulled out. They still loopin' and agin'."

"Until they"—Otto was hesitant saying it—"*die?*"

Grandma tilted her chin down, peered at them over the rims of her glasses. "We can only hope."

The boys somehow found the energy to pedal their bikes into the Gnarled Forest and onto a path leading straight to the creek. They'd used this path to catch the Queen of the Laughing Locusts as she was trying to get away and hatch more of her chuckling children. She'd thought crossing the creek would save her, but this path led to a hill at the creek's edge—a natural ramp. The boys used it to jump their bikes to the other side, where they eventually captured the Queen Locust.

Now they were counting on the Locust Queen's plan working better for them than it had for her.

The forest slowed Flux and the beast, as they were forced to knock down the ashen, leafless trees to keep up. It occurred to Otto that the creek might be time frozen. However, as they got closer, he heard the quiet roar of rushing water. Recalling the photo he'd taken, it made sense. The creek ran at the city's outside edge, so it was likely right outside of the photo's border. It didn't get caught in the time-stopping picture.

At the hill leading to the ramp, the boys halted. The path wasn't wide enough for two at a time.

"You first," said Otto.

"Why me?"

Sheed had saved him from toppling off his bike when the chase first started; he kind of owed him. Otto didn't want to admit that, so he said, "Because."

Then shoved Sheed down the hill.

Knowing better than to hesitate, Sheed pedaled into the descent, doubling his speed. At the bottom of the hill, he pedaled harder, shooting up that earthy incline.

"Arggghhh!" he screamed, going airborne, sailing over those eternally dangerous waters. His front tire tilted high; he imagined wings sprouting from the handlebars and jet fire shooting from his seat as his back tire touched down on the opposite side of the creek. He completed Maneuver #42 in a spectacular wheelie.

Sheed put his bike back on two wheels and spun to face his cousin, ready to cheer him on. That cheer got stuck in his throat. The ramp he'd used to jump the creek—just some dirt and roots over rushing water—was crumbling. The inclined edge, the part that made it such a good ramp, must've been weakened since they last used it. Chunky clods dislodged from the creek's bank and toppled into the water, swept into the loop.

Otto's neck was craned away, watching for Flux and the Time Suck, so he didn't see what Sheed saw. He didn't know the ramp was gone.

Flux and his beast crested the hill, right on top of Otto, who instinctively put his bike in motion, shooting down the path.

"No," Sheed screamed, too late.

Otto pedaled into the descent. Flux and the beast came down right behind him, fast, handling the hill with great agility; the beast could've licked Otto's back tire. Otto focused on the path ahead, the ramp.

Where is the ramp?! he thought, unable to slow down. Even if he dumped the bike, he'd either tumble into the creek or be caught by Flux. Another of Grandma's sayings came to mind: *stuck between a rock and a hard place.*

Maybe I can make it, he thought, rushing to the edge. Then realizing in the moment before leaving the ground that there was no way he'd make it. Not him *and* the bike.

Testing his own agility, he gripped his handlebars for leverage, then leapt, planting both feet on the bike seat. As the bike reached the creek bank, he released the handlebars and pushed off the seat with all his might, going airborne as his bike tipped and splashed into the water.

Sheed ran to creek's edge, arms outstretched, a catcher's stance.

Otto's legs pinwheeled, arms reaching for Sheed, the camera dangling from his neck. Both boys saw the truth.

He wasn't going to make it.

As strange as Logan County was, as often as its residents dealt with odd threats and weird occurrences and mysterious happenings, it wasn't all bad. Sometimes luck showed its hand.

Mr. Flux intended for the Time Suck to jump the creek and land on Sheed's side. The beast, perhaps recognizing the danger in the water, wasn't having it. It slid to a stop. Science fanatic Leen Ellison would've been happy to explain what happened next in the longest way possible, but it could be summarized by quoting Newton's First Law of Motion: *every object will remain at rest or in uniform motion in a straight line unless compelled to change its state by the action of an external force.*

Even though the beast stopped, Mr. Flux remained in motion, flying forward, losing his grip on the tufts of fur, shooting across the stream, colliding with Otto in midair.

The impact nudged Otto forward enough to grab Sheed's forearm. He didn't clear the creek completely, but fell onto the bank, dragging Sheed flat on his stomach. While Otto's legs dipped in the rushing water all the way to his calves, Mr. Flux fell in fully, stretching and flopping his limbs against the current.

"Pull me up," Otto said.

Sheed groaned. "No more Frosty Loops for you, yo!"

Mr. Flux shouted through the rushing current. "This isn't over, boys!"

Otto dragged his soaked feet from the water, climbing while Sheed pulled. His eyes were on Mr. Flux, still splashing, still threatening. As he was swept away, a pale gray, raisin-wrinkled hand emerged from the creek, and palmed Flux's face, as if to pull him under. Mr. Flux snarled and began fighting whoever that hand belonged to instead of the current. They both disappeared around a bend.

Otto remembered what Grandma said when he asked if people who never got pulled from the creek looped until they died. *We can only hope.*

He got himself up and away from that water in a hurry.

Sheed flopped on the creek bank. Eyes skyward, gasping. Across the creek, the duck-billed beast grazed, calm now that it wasn't at Flux's mercy.

"I think we gotta lose Maneuver #42," said Sheed.

Otto said, "Agreed." Then collapsed beside his cousin.

16
Epic. Fail.

AFTER A MUCH-NEEDED REST, Sheed got his bike upright and said, "We gotta get to town. We ain't catching Flux now, so we need to find that stranger. He knows way more than we do. He knows *maneuvers*."

That had been on Otto's mind a lot. How the stranger knew their maneuvers was definitely a mystery that needed solving. There was something else, though. Something the stranger said shortly after falling from his portal and getting into a fight with Flux.

Get back to the house. I got this.

He didn't say, "Run away!" Or, "Get home!"

Get back to the house.

The phrasing, it felt too . . . *familiar*. As if the stranger *knew* Grandma's house somehow, knew it more than a stranger should.

Or maybe Otto was reaching. He jotted down his concern, but didn't share it. Not yet.

Sheed said, "You ready?"

Otto said, "I don't have a bike."

"What do you think the handlebars are for?"

Sheed huffed hard, shoving the pedals, peering over Otto's shoulder at the road.

"You can't go faster?" Otto said.

"Are you serious?"

Otto wasn't serious. He allowed himself a little fun, messing with Sheed. There *was* a serious matter to consider. "What if we can't find him?"

"We fix this anyway." Sheed's certainty—with no plan—was comforting. Otto almost believed him.

They broke free of the Gnarled Forest onto asphalt, an easier effort for Sheed. They were sailing along about a mile from Fry. They passed a couple of frozen cars but saw no one else for most of the trip. A quarter mile from Fry, a couple of human-shaped silhouettes were visible at the forest border. The closer they got, the clearer the details. Was that . . . ?

Sheed said, "Oh . . ."

"Snap!" said Otto. Then, "Keep going. We can't do anything for them."

"No way."

Of course Sheed wasn't going to pass them. Or, rather, *her*.

They coasted to a stop a few feet from the pair. Otto hopped off the handlebars, and Sheed let the bike fall at his feet.

"I thought the day couldn't get any worse," said a frozen Victoria "Wiki" Ellison, one half of Otto and Sheed's (but mostly Otto's) local rivals.

Wiki was dark brown, with her glistening black hair cinched in a stiff ponytail. She wore a red and black plaid shirt, denim jeans cuffed at her calves, and Air Jordans. Always Air Jordans. Stuck a few paces behind her, with close-cropped hair, dark crescents of motor oil under her fingernails, in a flowery orange dress, with a loaded tool belt looped tight around her waist, was Wiki's twin sister, Evangeleen.

The Epic Ellison Girls.

The Ellisons were frozen mid-stride, on the run, Wiki's trusty bulging satchel cinched over her shoulder and trailing behind her. Evangeleen was stuck looking over her shoulder, a long wrench gripped in one fist. As usual, Sheed was drawn directly to her like a bee to a dandelion. "Hey, Leen."

"Hey, Sheed."

Otto rolled his eyes so hard, his head nearly tipped off his shoulders. "Heyyyyy, Leen!"

Sheed clenched his fists and gave Otto the evil eye, but did not stray from Evangeleen's side. Yuck.

"You two did this. Didn't you?" Wiki sniped, somehow making her voice sneer—her favorite expression—because her face couldn't.

"That doesn't seem very *scientific*, Wiki," Otto sneered back. "Where's your evidence?"

"That camera around your neck. And that you're not frozen."

That knocked Otto speechless. He struggled for an appropriate comeback.

Wiki said, "Please, stop trying to figure a way to outwit me. You can't. I know there's something off about that camera because it's put together wrong."

Sheed and Leen, somehow always in sync said, "What do you mean?"

"I mean it's supposed to look like a six-hundred-series instant camera, from Polaroid's most popular line. From a distance, yeah, it would pass, but up close it's *obviously* a bad facsimile."

That right there was part of the reason she was known as Wiki and why Otto kind of hated her. Rumor had it she read Wikipedia articles for fun. Otto and Sheed had crossed paths, and butted heads, with the Ellisons enough times to know that was only half of the story.

Wiki kept going. "There are no seams, no screws; the

flash is on the wrong side. I would ask if the thing even works, but you're lugging it around when you don't have your own bike. Tells me it's of some importance. Given that everything seems to be frozen but you two, I bet that camera's got something to do with what's happening. Tell me I'm wrong."

Otto wanted nothing more than to tell her she was wrong. For once. It was so unfair. She wasn't a deductive mastermind *like him*.

She *was* a deductive mastermind, he supposed, but her gift wasn't honed from training her mind for acute observation. She was *born* with a computer-like brain.

Wiki Ellison never forgot anything. Ever.

Not those Wikipedia articles she combed through, not anything she ever saw.

There was a word for it. *Idyllic*? No. Not *idiotic* (he'd love to toss that one at Wiki, though.)

"*Eidetic*," she said.

Otto's breathing quickened. Could she read minds, too? "How did . . . I didn't . . ."

"Your facial expression. It's like reading a book. You had the precise look from when I first told you about my memory. The left side of your mouth twitched up. Your eyes flicked to the right. It's your jealous tick."

"I am *not* jealous."

"Your eyes just flicked left, and you're frowning. That's your liar tick."

Otto sidestepped from her line of sight so she couldn't analyze his face anymore.

Wiki said, "Rude."

Sheed somehow managed to pull his eyes from Leen and followed her gaze. She was stuck looking behind them, far back into the Gnarled Forest where a pair of gleaming red lenses flared ten feet above the forest floor. They were set in a huge, dark, shadowy *something* that Sheed couldn't —and didn't want to—see. "What is that?"

"My newest robot." Leen was the tinkerer of the pair. The boys had seen her build fantastic—sometimes frightening—things. Some people in Logan thought Evangeleen Ellison was a junior mad scientist. Sheed always found her happy and pleasant. A *glad* scientist.

Though her inventions were known to get loose from time to time.

This one was bigger than most, with the jagged angles and uneven limbs that were Leen's signature, since she built most of her machines out of whatever found junk she got her hands on. This particular invention lunged with one arm stretched toward the girls; it seemed to be chasing the Ellisons.

Sheed asked, "Uhhhhh, what happened here?"

Leen said, "I've been working on some new artificial intelligence protocols. Specifically, tag. As in 'tag, you're it.' I was able to program the rules of the game well enough, but I didn't account for the robot's strength."

Otto said, "So . . . ?"

"Whatever the robot tags, the robot destroys," said Wiki, her words sharp. "And we're 'it.'"

"You don't have to sound like that," said Leen. "I can hear the judgment in your voice."

Wiki cut her off. "We can talk about it some other time, sis. Otto, sweetie, since today's biggest problem isn't the

114

robot that wants to crush me and my shortsighted sibling, please tell me you're close to figuring out the frozen time thing."

Making sure she couldn't see his face, he said, "We are."

"Uh-huh. So, you got a way to unfreeze me and Leen?"

Unfreezing people required the assistance of a Clock Watcher, and since none were present, Otto said, "Not at the moment."

"As I suspected. It's really too bad. I'm certain you could use our help on this. Or we could just do it for you. Maybe grab our fourth Key to the City in the process."

That jab stung Otto to his very core.

Wiki said, "Are you making your jealous face again?"

"Girl, bye! Sheed, let's go." Otto stomped back to the bike, while Sheed made his final googly eyes.

"Bye, Sheed," said Leen.

"Bye, Leen." His fingertips grazed her hand.

Otto threw up in his mouth a little.

"Sheed! Let's go find the stranger." And definitely grab a third Key to the City in the process.

He could go back to living with a tie. For now.

17

Your Mama Named You That?

"YOU KNOW"—SHEED WORKED THE pedals easily now, like he'd gotten a boost of unexpected energy—"the girls might be able to help. They're pretty good with Logan County weirdness."

"They can't move, so they can't help. Drop it."

"I'm just saying, Wiki and Leen see things differently than us. It's not like we never teamed up before."

Otto, scowling, twisted on his handlebar seat, rocking the bike.

"Hey." Sheed fought to maintain their balance. "Stop moving."

"We didn't team up with the Ellisons. *You* invited Leen because you want her to be your girlfriend and left me dealing with Wiki getting in the way."

Bashful, Sheed said, "That's not the way I remember it."

"We don't need their help. We're legends. Legends are better than epics."

"Actually, they're kind of like synonyms. I checked the thesaurus."

"Shut up."

They spoke of the Epic Ellisons no more as they sailed back into Fry—same scene, different angle. All frozen everything. They went to the building where the stranger had yelled their own maneuver at them. Big Apple Bakery, named so because Miss Remica, the owner, was from New York City and used really big apples in her tarts and pies and turnovers that Otto loved more than any sweet treat around (don't tell Grandma!). Climbing the fire escape to the roof, they found no stranger and no clue of where he might've gone. From this high view, they looked over the unmoving city under a fixed bright sun and wondered what they could possibly do next.

"We don't know where to even begin to look." Sheed flopped on his butt, dog-tired.

Otto reviewed his notes. "Maybe we go back to Harkness Hill. Check the area where the stranger's portal appeared. There might be evidence."

"I'm going to need a break first." Sheed said, breathing hard.

He looked more tired than Otto had ever seen him. The double-bike ride must have worn him down.

Otto said, "I'll pedal us out there. You can rest on the handlebars."

"You're extra bossy today, cuz."

"I'm sorry if frozen time is getting in the way of your napping."

This was about to be a fight. The boys had learned to sense when they were coming on. Sometimes it was words. Yelled words, mean words. In the worst moments, they wrestled and threw punches. Never around Grandma because she'd make them scrub floors, and iron drapes, and weed the garden until they were too exhausted to scuffle. No Grandma around, though.

Sheed, slowly, a little stiff, stood up. "The time freeze wouldn't have happened if you didn't take that camera from Flux."

"All of a sudden, Logan County strangeness is my fault, huh?"

"Today it is."

Otto stuffed his notebook in his pocket, dropped his backpack, and clenched his fists. Sheed bent his knees the way Muhammad Ali did in old videos. They drew near.

The rooftop door swung open on squealing rusty hinges, snatching their attention.

From inside the shadowy stairwell, the stranger emerged with that bucking sack hoisted on his shoulder and a half-eaten turnover in hand. Through a mouthful of apple goodness, he said, "Hey, fellas. Been waiting on you."

The boys remained on guard.

He strolled closer, taking another chomp of his turnover before kneeling and placing the sack on the rooftop. It—or whoever was in it—arched like an inchworm, attempting to creep away. The stranger planted a boot on the sack's loose edge so it couldn't go far. He devoured the rest of his pastry, licked crumbs off his fingers when he was done. "I forgot how good these things are."

"Who are you?" Otto demanded.

The stranger's reflective goggles settled on Otto. "My name"—his dark, scraggly beard split in a smile—"is TimeStar."

Sheed said, "TimeStar? Your mama named you *TimeStar?*"

His smile faltered. "Uh, no. That's my public identity. My real name is a secret. Because I'm a hero when I'm from."

He said hero. And *when* I'm from, not *where*. Otto, suspicious, said, "You're a time-traveling superhero?"

TimeStar took a wide-legged stance, planted his fists on his hips, and tilted his head toward the sky. A classic superhero pose. "Can't you tell?"

Not really. Although he did fall out of a portal, and his clothes looked futuristic.

Sheed said, "How'd you know about Maneuver #42?"

TimeStar abandoned his pose. "When I'm from,

everybody knows about the Legendary Alston Boys of Logan County. Your maneuvers are well documented."

"When is that exactly?" Otto asked.

"The year 2211."

"Why are you here?"

TimeStar leveled his gaze at Otto. "A sightseeing trip. And"—he dropped his eyes, became a bit shy—"I wanted to see the Legendary Alston Boys of Logan County in action. That Laughing Locust adventure is all the rage in my time. There's—goodness—at least three major motion pictures about it."

Otto's jaw dropped. "There are movies about us in the future?"

"Sure. And Holo-streams, and virtual reality games. Tons of stuff. Traveling to see you live is a very popular vacation excursion."

Otto said, "You mean other time travelers have been back to watch us? How come we've never seen them?"

"The Time Bureau dictates that we stay hidden. We cannot, under any circumstances, change things in the past. So you wouldn't have seen any of my fellow travelers."

Sheed held up one finger, skeptical. "You're not hiding, though. And why are you here now? The Laughing Locusts were months ago."

TimeStar shrugged. "Best guess? This time freeze thing disrupted my travel route. Spit me out here unexpectedly.

As far as the hiding, since I'm a superhero—one of the best, mind you—I'm willing to improvise, given today's unusual circumstances."

Sheed said, "Excuse us."

He turned toward the ledge, motioned for Otto to do the same. Otto joined him, occasionally flicking glances over his shoulder at the self-proclaimed hero.

"You buying any of that?" Sheed asked.

"It sounds ridiculous. Like something we'd make up on our way to the comic book store," Otto said. "Mostly."

"Why mostly?"

"He did fall from hole in the sky. Time's weird today. A time traveler in the mix isn't so far-fetched, is it?"

Sheed's face twisted. "*TimeStar*, though?"

"Yeah, that's stupid. But how'd he know about our maneuvers if at least some of what he's saying isn't true?"

Sheed had no good answer. "Play along?"

"Might as well."

They faced the so-called TimeStar. Otto pointed at the writhing sack by the time traveler's feet. "What's going on there?"

His smile stretched, full and bright. "I brought you a present."

The human-size sack kept trying to slink away. Time-Star yanked it back and undid the crisscrossed ties that kept it sealed. When the fabric uncinched wide enough, a blue-gray hand shot out, talon-like nails curving from the fingertips.

Otto and Sheed screamed and scrambled backwards.

"It's okay, guys," TimeStar said. "She looks much meaner than she is."

She?

The boys took cautious steps forward while TimeStar opened the sack fully. A mop of dusty hair threaded with spiderwebs popped free. Yellow eyes peered from between the ragged split strands, and a hiss spilled from a mouth full of fangs. She wore a frilly black dress that appeared scorched at the edges. A dense swampy mist seeped out of

the bag, and her wrists were bound with several loops of twine.

This was one of the stampeding Clock Watchers they'd spotted from Mr. Archie's window earlier. She'd been super creepy, floating on a bed of fog. Otto believed TimeStar on this one thing: there was no way this Clock Watcher could be as mean as she looked. Still . . .

"You kidnapped her?" Sheed said, horrified.

"No," said TimeStar, "I *apprehended* her before she could do more damage. When I found her, she was in Sunshine Cemetery working on some sort of spell around all the graves. I don't know exactly what she planned, but she'd set up a big banner that said WELCOME BACK! I figured it was best not to let her see that through."

"A spell?" said Otto.

The supposed time traveler knelt beside her, said, "Tell them who you are."

Sheed stiffened, expecting some monstrous, cackling squeal of a voice.

"Hi!" she said, her voice as calm and plain as their social studies teacher. "I'm Witching Hour. You've probably met a few of my Clock Watcher colleagues."

TimeStar waved her on. "Tell them what you did."

"I made that." Witching Hour pointed at the camera around Otto's neck. "Probably a little too well. Wouldn't you say?"

18
Witching Hour

OTTO RAISED THE CAMERA, once again considering the impossible way it was put together and the impossible thing it had done.

ENTRY #58

DEDUCTION: A magical camera—built by a witch—makes perfect sense in Logan County's special imperfect way.

Sheed said, "You're called Witching Hour?"

"That's correct."

"Are you a witch, or are you an hour?"

"Both."

"Like the way the Golden Hours are time *and* stylists?" Otto offered.

"Exactly."

Sheed shook his head. "Whatever. Why did you make that camera?"

Witching Hour threw her head back and cackled, a harsh, gargling laugh that echoed over Fry. They all recoiled. The laugh cut out abruptly, and she returned to the calm voice. "Apologies, I can't always control the laugh. Anyhow, a naughty being sought me out at my designated time. I was required to help him."

"Flux," TimeStar said.

As if we didn't know that's who she was talking about, Otto thought, annoyed by Captain Obvious.

Sheed asked, "Is Mr. Flux a Clock Watcher like you and the rest?"

"No. He is most definitely not part of our family. He is a malicious manifestation from outside of our natural realm." She burped another short cackle.

Sheed said, "What realm did he come from?"

"The only one capable of conjuring such chaos. Yours. A human created Mr. Flux."

Otto followed that up with, "What human?"

Witching Hour poked a talon into her mouth, considering. "I do not know."

Otto said, "How do we know you're telling the truth?"

"I always tell the truth," she said earnestly. "I'm all about mischief, and nothing causes more mischief than the truth.

But you already know that, or else the two of you wouldn't be keeping so many secrets. Am I right?"

Witching Hour had wild eyes that seemed to move independently of each other, never focusing on any one thing. So, Otto wasn't clear on her last statement. "There are three of us. Which two do you mean?"

Her only response was a fanged grin.

Frowns all around, and Otto's immediate reaction was to deny her accusation. But . . . they already didn't believe TimeStar. If they were right, he was definitely keeping secrets. He wanted to believe that Sheed didn't keep things from him; only he'd never admitted his crush on Leen Ellison. Could that be one of the secrets she spoke of?

I'm not keeping any secrets, Otto thought. That wasn't true either, was it? His cheeks burned with embarrassment. There he was, lying to himself. Proving Witching Hour right.

Sheed said, "Come on, lady. What kind of secrets are you talking about?"

Another cackle from Witching Hour, full of extra glee. "I said I always tell the truth. I did not say I always *tell*. Secrets are the best truths, and silence is always an option."

"You're not going to tell us any more about Mr. Flux, then?"

She whipped her bird's nest hair about, a vicious head-shake that sent dust and bugs airborne. "Oh no, I'll tell you all I know about him. I don't like the circumstances we find ourselves in any more than you. Just because I was compelled to help him doesn't mean I'm compelled to keep *his* secrets. Gather 'round, and let ole Witchy tell you a tale!"

Otto sat. Sheed followed. TimeStar remained standing, and also suspiciously quiet throughout this exchange. If he really was a hero, why was he letting them do all the work?

Though her wrists were cinched with twine, she cupped her hands together; they bulged and pulsed, as if she had a fidgety mouse trapped between her palms, and white light leaked between her fingers. When she spread her hands, her palms side by side, a tiny globe—the size of a tennis ball—floated an inch above her gray-blue skin.

Witching Hour, as pleasant in her unpleasantness as can be, said, "We share the world. Us Clock Watchers and you humans. Mostly, we're unaware of each other, since me and my colleagues tend to operate behind the scenes—in what you might call a different dimension—and are very focused on our tasks. You only recognize us as your day dragging when you're bored or flying by when you're having fun. We dictate when you go to sleep, eat dinner, or start a new season. Even though your measly, inadequate human perceptions don't normally allow you to see us in our true forms, you know that we're always there."

Sheed raised his hand like they were at school, a question on his mind.

Witching Hour said, "Except when you go to the bath-room. That would be uncomfortable for everyone."

Sheed lowered his hand.

"I know that seems very crowded," she continued, "and sometimes it is. A Second Guesser might ride on a Minute Man's shoulders, while the Minute Man rides Dinner Hour piggyback. A Second Guesser and a Minute Man tried to jump on my shoulders once, but a spider crawled from my hair and scared them off. That spider's name was Stan."

"Is Stan important in this story?" Otto asked, taking notes.

"A good spider is always important. Remember that, boys."

All righty, then.

Witching Hour's toothy grin shrank a bit on the next part. "The thing you have to understand is even though we share the same world, humans and Clock Watchers never truly mingled before, not like we are now. Until Mr. Flux broke the rules and changed everything."

"With your help." Sheed wasn't letting her off the hook.

"Us Clock Watchers have unyielding natures. When he approached me with mischief in his heart at the exact stroke of midnight, I couldn't say no."

Sheed said, "Hey, TimeStar, what do you think about all this?"

TimeStar fidgeted, twisting a single dreadlock around

his pointer finger. "I think you two should listen. While I also listen, I mean."

What is his deal? thought Otto.

Witching Hour continued, "This part of your world, your Logan County, is different than most places. If there's a location for our respective dimensions to crisscross in unexpected and dangerous ways, it's here. Mr. Flux was the victim of such an occurrence. He is not a man, and he is not a Clock Watcher. He is a Missed Opportunity."

The boys shot each other puzzled looks. Otto said, "He's mad because he missed out on something?"

"No! He *is* the opportunity that was missed. A bitter castoff. Someone could've done something, but they didn't. A common occurrence, really. But, in this strange place, common can become uncommon in the blink of an eye. Correct?"

The boys and TimeStar nodded. This was Logan County.

Witching Hour said, "Mr. Flux found himself trapped between humans and time. Ignored by people and Clock Watchers, he became rage-filled and perhaps a bit insane. He seethed and festered and plotted, waiting for a time and the means to strike at us all. Today.

"He sought me out, asked for passage into the human dimension and a tool to exact his revenge. I didn't *want* to do it; my strict nature as a troublemaker compelled me. But, being as mischievous as I am, I built a safeguard into the device so its initial use had to be triggered by a Clock Watcher or human. I knew none of my colleagues would do the dirty deed . . . We're too busy. And I thought perhaps any humans he came across would be way too smart to fall for his schemes."

Otto and Sheed suddenly found their sneakers very interesting.

Witching Hour clapped her palms together, smooshing the globe. "Clearly I was mistaken."

"Why's he doing this, though?" Sheed, grim and scared, said. "What does he want?"

"To ensure no one in Fry ever misses an opportunity again. If you haven't noticed, he succeeded."

19
Last Place You Look

"NO WAY!" SHEED POPPED UP, tired of story time, tired
of doing nothing. (Truthfully, just plain tired. He was sore
and still a little winded from all of the day's activity, though
now was no time for rest.) "You're acting like he won. We
got news for you, Witching Hour. He's done. We tossed
him in the creek. Now tell us how to unfreeze time."

For the first time, even after admitting her role in today's
mess, Witching Hour seemed shamefaced. She pressed her
palms together again; more light leaked between her fingers. "That is the most mischievous part of his plan. Only
he can undo it."

Suddenly, throwing Mr. Flux into the Eternal Creek
did not seem like the victory Sheed had thought it was. If
he was the only one who could fix this, and he was stuck in
a creek loop . . .

Witching Hour cackled again. "Him, or perhaps the

person who created him in the first place." She spread her palms, and what floated there was not a globe or some other fantastic visual. It was scissors.

The freshly cut twine fell away from her wrists.

"Get her," Otto said, too late.

Sneaky quick, Witching Hour sprang to her feet and darted between Otto and Sheed.

"Hey!" TimeStar said with jerking awareness, like he'd fallen asleep on his feet.

Some reflexes for a superhero, Otto thought.

She reached the bakery ledge, faced them. "I'm sorry, boys. You seem nice, but I wasn't lying about mischief being my nature. Just do us all a favor and fix this mess so I can get back to my regularly scheduled programs. Witching Hour gotta witch." She gave a cutesy finger wave. "Toodles."

Witching Hour leapt off the building.

Otto, Sheed, and TimeStar rushed the ledge, all afraid of seeing a splatted Witching Hour on the sidewalk below. She wasn't splatted; she zoomed away on her bed of swamp fog.

TimeStar smacked his own forehead. Rushed to the fire escape. "I'm going after her."

"Wait!" the boys said.

"We might need her." He swung one leg onto the rusty ladder, then the other, and descended. "I'll handle it. You go find A.M. and P.M., and I'll catch up later."

TimeStar was gone.

"How did we let her get away?" Sheed said, mad at himself.

"How did we let *him* get away?" said Otto, also mad, though he stared awful hard at Sheed.

"What? Don't look at me like that."

"Did you hear what he said? He told us to find A.M. and P.M. How did he know we call them that?"

"Maybe all our stuff really is in the historical records where he comes from. That would mean he's not lying about the future. That's good news, right?"

Otto wasn't so sure.

They left the bakery roof and returned to the last place they saw the Golden Hours. Fry High.

It was slow climbing the hill to the high school. Sheed dragged, opting to walk beside his bike rather than ride it, meaning Otto walked, too. How long had they been at this? There was no true way to tell. With time frozen, the sun didn't move. The sky didn't change. They could have been chasing Clock Watchers for days.

The school library, crammed with Clock Watchers the last time they were there, was utterly deserted. No A.M., or P.M., or anyone.

"Now what?" Sheed said, catching his breath.

Otto had considered this possibility, as well as all the

things they'd learned from Witching Hour. He consulted his notes, keying in on one thing in particular.

"The witch said only Mr. Flux, or maybe the person who created him, could fix this."

"Right," said Sheed, wheezy.

"So why did Mr. Flux come *here*?"

Sheed pointed at Otto's chest. "He wanted that camera. That's what he chased us all over town for."

No. That wasn't right. Otto checked all the notes he'd taken since the encounter and explained his reasoning. "He didn't know we were here when he came to the library. He only went for the camera after he saw us. Remember? We were hiding. He came here to mess with Father Time." He jotted more notes. "Over the yearbooks."

ENTRY #63

DEDUCTION: There's something in the yearbooks that he was worried about.

ADDITIONAL DEDUCTION: If Mr. Flux is worried about it, it might help us.

Sheed said, "You gonna tell me what's cooking in that brain of yours?"

"Good news or bad news first?"

"Good news."

"We're going to rest here awhile." Otto tried to sound cheery.

"What's the bad news?"

"It's only bad if you don't like reading senior quotes."

Sheed sighed, quick counting the dozens of yearbooks scattered on the floor. "I'll take the even years, you take the odd."

With no way to know how much time passed, Sheed measured his effort in the number of yearbooks he'd painstakingly searched page by page. So far, he'd done four. Otto was up to five. Sheed had had to stop and suck his thumb, though. Paper cut. "This is boring. And painful. What are we looking for?"

"I already told you, we'll know when we see it." Otto wasn't sure that was true. He hoped it was something obvious, something really helpful. Not more nonsense wisdom (YOLO!) from people like Sylvester the Wise. Whatever that something was, they hadn't found it yet.

Grandma always said, *Whatever you need is always in the last place you look.*

It sounded deep, but it really meant that once you found it, why would you look in more places?

He tossed a yearbook into the pile between them.

They'd started with the most recent and worked backwards. Sheed's four and Otto's five meant they'd gone through the last nine years of Fry High students. In many cases, they saw students in all four years of their time at the school, from braces to bifocals, pimples to perms. Otto found that horribly inefficient.

"Why don't we look at the seniors and the freshmen only?" Otto suggested. "We won't see the same people as much."

"Until the freshmen become seniors."

"I didn't say the system was perfect."

Sheed sucked his teeth. Otto resisted the urge to throw a yearbook at him. This never-ending day was getting to them.

Grabbing the next yearbook off the stack, droopy-eyed Sheed leafed through a few pages, his head bobbing like he might doze off, before rocking forward on his knees, thrusting the yearbook at Otto. "Look!"

Otto leaned in, not particularly hopeful until he saw the picture within the grid of bow ties and strapless gowns that filled the senior section. It was a boy named Donald O'Doyle. Pale, with a sinister grin and familiar blue eyes. His senior quote read, "Hey, Butthead!"

Otto's hunch about the yearbooks had been right. He'd save his I-told-you-so for a later date.

Because Donald O'Doyle was Mr. Flux.

20
O'Soiled

OR RATHER, DONALD O'DOYLE, who'd graduated from Fry High ten years ago, *looked just like* Mr. Flux.

Better known as Mr. O'Doyle these days (or Mr. *O'Soiled* by those brave enough to whisper the nickname whenever he walked by), he was the mean janitor at D. Franklin Middle School, who tripped kids in the cafeteria if he saw them spill ketchup or salt. When they fell face first —always when teachers weren't watching—he'd say, "Now there's a new stain on my floor."

Though Otto and Sheed knew him well—and knew to avoid him—they couldn't have placed him as Mr. Flux's double before. Back-in-the-day Donald O'Doyle looked like Mr. Flux, skinny and pale. Current Mr. O'Doyle was much larger, with less hair and red peeling skin from sunburns. Time had changed him a lot.

He lived in a shabby, rundown house on the edge of Fry,

with old tires, a rusty wheelbarrow, a condemned birdhouse, an airplane toilet, and other trash in the yard. Nobody knew how all that stuff got there, just that every so often it became *more* instead of *less*. It was as if he hated cleaning up after the kids at D. Franklin Middle so much, he refused to clean up after himself when he finished his workday. Otto and Sheed had heard people call his yard "the second town dump" and laugh. Maybe they'd laughed, too, even though that wasn't very nice.

The boys stood outside his gray, peeling picket fence. Sheed leaned his bike against a plank, and the rotting wood broke from his slight touch, falling into the cluttered yard.

"Wow, not even frozen time can keep this place from getting junkier," said Sheed.

Otto fished the incriminating yearbook from his backpack, flipped to the page featuring a young Mr. O'Doyle looking exactly like Mr. Flux, and said, "It can't be a coincidence. If they look so much alike, Mr. O'Doyle has to be the person Witching Hour told us about. The one who created Mr. Flux and can stop the time freeze."

"Maybe," Sheed said. "Hopefully."

Otto stepped into the yard. Sheed followed. They weaved through so many more oddities than what could be spotted from the road. There was a dented punching bag with sand spilling from its ripped side. A speedboat motor. A paper shredder. And so on.

At the front door, the boys leaned close to the wood, listening for . . . they didn't know. The sound they heard was unexpected. Inside, someone was crying softly.

Otto knocked on the door. "Hello?"

The crying stopped, and that familiar, crackly mean voice shouted. "Who is it? Who's there?"

"Mr. O'Doyle, can we come in?"

The angry man said, "No! Absolutely not! I don't want you tracking dirt in my house."

Sheed shoved the door open. "Time's frozen. What's he gonna do?"

He was right, of course. There was no threat to contend with, no weapon to dodge. Otto took a reluctant lead and crossed the threshold into Mr. O'Doyle's home. He'd assumed it would be as junky as the yard. Quite the opposite. It was as neat as Grandma's house. So neat, it felt like O'Doyle needed *more* stuff.

Inside the foyer, there was only a slim iron coat rack and a short table where house keys sat. In the living room a couch, a fireplace, and a coffee table with the latest issues of *Good Housekeeping* on it.

Mr. O'Doyle spoke through his soft sobbing. "Whoever you are, please, please don't hurt me."

Wasn't that something? He terrorized kids at their school for minor messes; now he was the minor mess.

Trekking through his space, the boys craned their necks,

taking in any details they could. There weren't many. Not even family photos. You couldn't take a step in Grandma's house without running across pictures of family from all over, like Grandma's brothers and sisters and her nieces and nephews—who all lived in places way less strange than Logan these days. And, of course, photos of Otto's and Sheed's parents were plentiful, despite their ability to make Grandma and the boys sad from time to time. Even on the sad days, all those pictures gave a feeling that was missing in Mr. O'Doyle's house. His home felt incomplete, and that was more sad than sad pictures, somehow.

They entered the kitchen where mean Mr. O'Doyle sat in the only chair next to a small dining table. He was dressed neatly in pleated slacks, a clean lavender shirt, with his normally dingy hair combed and shiny with gel. They couldn't see his face because his back was to them. And he couldn't see them, even if they circled to his front, because the newspaper he held was opened wide, blocking his view.

"Who's there?" he demanded. "Who is violating my home?"

Otto reached as if to remove the paper, but Sheed stopped him with a slight head shake. Best if he didn't know who they were.

Making his voice comically deep, enough that Otto clamped a hand over his own mouth so as not to laugh, Sheed spoke in a gruff tone similar to their favorite movie superhero, the masked vigilante ArmadilloMan. "What have you and Mr. Flux done to bring this terrible plight on Logan County?"

"I don't know what you're talking about. Mr. Who? You're scaring me."

Sheed believed Mr. O'Doyle was afraid. From all he'd seen, mean people scared the easiest when things weren't in their control. But there had to be a connection between him and Mr. Flux for them to look so similar. Maybe if they distracted him from his fear, he'd be better able to help them find the connection.

The place was spotless. Every thing that could shine— faucet, refrigerator handle, stainless steel spatula—shined. Everything that could smell like lemon cleaner emitted citrus notes. No wonder he got so mad when kids made messes at school. Mr. O'Doyle was a neat freak. Except for his yard. Sheed wondered if talking about that might make him less afraid and more like the Mr. O'Doyle they were used to. An angry motormouth.

"Why's the outside of your house so junky?" Sheed asked.

Sheed? Otto mouthed.

Sheed mouthed back, *I wanna know.*

Mr. O'Doyle seemed flustered by the question. He spoke fast, irritated. "The yard? I can't do anything with that. When I bought the house, I tried. Every time I cleaned, I'd come out the next day and more stuff would be there. I thought kids from the high school were throwing things over the fence. The airplane toilet seemed a little too heavy for teenagers though. Can you please tell me why I can't move?"

Sheed said, "Why don't you ask your buddy, Mr. Flux?" He gave Otto a sly thumbs-up. He was using those tight interrogation skills, like on Grandma's cop shows.

"I don't know who that is. Who are *you*, for that matter?"

Otto got in on the act. Turning the yearbook to Mr. O'Doyle's page, he made his interrogation voice the opposite of Sheed's. Low and squeaky. "Do you know who this is?"

He pushed the book between the newspaper and O'Doyle's eyes.

"Why do you have my yearbook? Are you book thieves?"

"No," said Sheed. "We're here to fix time. But we need to know how you created Mr. Flux."

"I already told you I don't know that name."

Otto said, "He looks just like you. You not knowing each other defies all deductions."

"The only thing I know is I was reading my morning paper when all of a sudden I couldn't move. I've been staring at this same article on grass watering ordinances for I don't know how long. Why is this happening?" Mr. O'Doyle started crying again, a strange and strained sound, a frightener frightened.

The boys retreated into his living room to discuss

strategy. Hushed and confused, Sheed said, "I think he's telling the truth."

Otto said, "Me too. He really does seem like he's been stuck all day. If he knew anything that would help us, he would've said so."

"I also think you're right."

"Does it hurt when you say that?"

Sheed punched him in the shoulder. "He doesn't look like Mr. Flux for no reason. So what's up?"

"What if he doesn't *know* he created Flux? Like O'Doyle missed the opportunity, and Mr. Flux just happened while his back was turned, or something."

"Maybe." Sheed stretched the word out with doubt.

"We're back to having no clues, though."

"We can still go looking for A.M. and P.M. Or TimeSt—"

Something crashed outside.

They approached the window, bending O'Doyle's blinds wide enough to peer out. For the second time on that frozen day, they didn't need to look further for whatever clue, obstacle, or plain old terror came next.

A drenched and angry-looking Mr. Flux was knocking aside any and every piece of yard junk between him and the front door, on his way inside.

For a visit that seemed anything but friendly.

21

Giants and Mice

"MANEUVER #22," THE BOYS SAID at the same time.

Sheed leapt into a narrow space behind the couch. Seeing no available closets, Otto shimmied behind the drapes. Both boys were barely settled before the door blew inward, cascading across the foyer floor in splinters as if obliterated by a stick of dynamite. Mr. Flux, dripping and snarling, called, "Donnie! Oh, Donnie Boy!"

"Now, who is this?" Mr. O'Doyle called, extra shaky.

"Your old friend Mr. Flux. I've had some unexpected distractions, but I've been looking forward to this visit for a long time."

So they do know each other, Otto thought.

Mr. O'Doyle immediately contradicted Otto's assumption. "I don't know you, sir. I told that to the others, too."

Mr. Flux's glee fizzled. There was a mighty tear—Flux

ripping the newspaper from O'Doyle's clenched hands. "What others? Who?"

"I couldn't see them. One sounded like a giant, the other sounded like a mouse."

"Clock. Watchers." Mr. Flux's disgusted tone was similar to Sheed's when the boy said, "Creamed. Spinach."

Though relieved that Mr. O'Doyle hadn't seen them and couldn't tell Mr. Flux exactly who'd been asking about him, a new fear arose for Sheed. This house wasn't as spotless as it seemed. There was plenty of dust behind the couch. The itchy-nose, watery-eye kind. The kind that could only be countered with a sneeze. Any noise, at all, would alert Mr. Flux, and though he'd somehow managed to climb from the Eternal Creek, he probably wouldn't be very nice to the boys responsible for dunking him in it. Sheed rubbed his nose vigorously, fighting the tickle.

Behind the drapes, Otto had a different problem. He wanted to *see* Mr. Flux and Mr. O'Doyle side by side. To compare, and take notes, and understand if there were more deductions to be made. Because somehow, someway, they had the same face, changed by time and age, but the same still.

That felt important.

Slinking from behind the drapes, he tiptoed toward the doorway to the kitchen where Flux and O'Doyle spoke. He put the camera and yearbook aside, then lowered to his round belly and scooted closer to the conversation, with his notepad in hand.

Sheed had shifted slightly, trying to escape the frolicking dust bunnies in his hiding space, and saw Otto going *toward the bad guy!* He waved his hands, frantic but silent, while screaming in his head, *Stop! Are you crazy?*

Otto ignored him.

Despite being sopping wet, Mr. Flux had managed to hang on to his stovepipe hat. His limbs seemed stretched, even more so than when they last saw him, the way a sweater sagged after Grandma pulled it from the washer but before she put it in the dryer.

Mr. Flux said, "Donny, you sly dog. You've really made something of yourself, haven't you?"

"Well, I'm quite proud of my home. Except the yard. As I explained to the others, it's like junk falls from the sky."

"Do you still pick on the weak and helpless, Donny? Are you proud of that, too?"

"I —" Mr. O'Doyle stammered, "I'm unsure what you're referring to."

In a booming voice that made Otto freeze and made Sheed want to snatch his cousin and run, Mr. Flux said, *"Fourscore and seven years ago . . . Peter was still a loser, everybody knows!* Does that sound familiar, Donny boy?"

"I — I don't —" Mr. O'Doyle did not sound convincing.

"How about *Peter Peter Poo-Poo Eater*? Or—this is a good one—*Smells-like-feet-Pete*? Aren't those funny? Don't you want to die laughing?"

"No! I didn't. I mean, I don't want to."

"You were a nasty little twerp, weren't you, Donny Boy? A nasty twerp who grew into a mean man. I've seen you."

"Whatever you think you saw—"

"I don't *think*, Donny. I once saw you trip a little girl because she dropped crumbs from her peanut butter and jelly. Did you make up a name for her? Something hilarious like the classic *Pete Big Brain, the Pee-Pee Stain*? Please don't tell me you stopped making up names for people. I would've thought you had a future in poetry. So clever."

Mr. O'Doyle's soft crying became sobbing. "I'm sorry. Please don't hurt me."

"Hurt you? Why would I do that? I'm here *because* of you. You and your clever names inspired my birth. You're almost like my dad."

Otto wrote much of this down, underlining the word *almost*. A big deduction was forming. They needed to get out of there.

Waving at Sheed, then motioning toward the door, Otto grabbed all he'd come with and crawled toward the exit, low and silent. Sheed, still rubbing his nose, followed. They made it to the foyer and through the destroyed entrance, tiptoeing around shards from the shattered door. About to have a clean getaway.

Sheed sneezed.

"What is that?" Mr. Flux said.

The boys split, diving into the yard, each ducking behind some large, odd piece of junk. Otto was behind an industrial cement mixer. Sheed knelt by the deflated folds of an orange bouncy house.

Though they couldn't see him, Mr. Flux made his presence on O'Doyle's porch known. "Is that you, Clock Watchers? There's nothing you can do to stop me. Your powers are useless now that time's no factor. And the numbers of your kind who stand against me dwindle. I have won. I would say take your time choosing your next steps, but I've already taken the time. Haven't I?"

Splinters crunched under his feet as he strolled back to resume torturing O'Doyle. He moved with confidence. No concern for anyone at all. Maybe he really couldn't be stopped.

Staying low, Otto snuck to Sheed's hiding spot, linked elbows, and led him through the collapsed section of fence. They retrieved the bike and slinked away from O'Doyle and his ghastly, villainous look-alike. They ran a full hundred yards and ducked into a neighbor's backyard, where a frozen dog barked at them. That noise wouldn't do, so they kept moving through other yards, around playhouses, and past trampolines until they were back to a road far away from Flux.

Sheed walked the bike. Otto flipped through the yearbook, playing out a hunch.

"What was that back there?" Sheed said.

"A big clue," Otto said. "Did you hear Mr. Flux say O'Doyle was *almost* like his dad?"

"Almost." Sheed nodded. "So, Mr. O'Doyle isn't who created Flux, but he had something to do with it. Maybe that's why they look so much alike?"

"That's what I deduce. Mr. Flux kept going on about O'Doyle's mean nicknames. Peter this, and Peter that. We know a Peter. Or, rather, a Petey."

Otto showed Sheed the yearbook pages he'd dog-eared. A school photo of a scrawny, pimply-faced kid in the freshman section. Other photos, too. Science Club. Math Club. Drama Club. Peter Thunkle, the butt of O'Doyle's mean names was none other than Petey, their dour clerk friend from Archie's Hardware Store.

"Get out!" Sheed dropped his bike and snatched the book.

Otto asked, "Do you notice anything in that Drama Club photo?"

Sheed scrutinized it. A cast photo, with the players

dressed in their costumes from their production of *Abraham Lincoln*.

Abe Lincoln was played by none other than Donald O'Doyle. In his black suit and stovepipe hat, he didn't just resemble Mr. Flux in this photo; he *was* Mr. Flux.

At least to a tormented Petey, in overalls with a bulky tool belt on his waist, whom Donny Boy held in a headlock at the moment the picture was snapped.

Sheed closed the yearbook. "So, if Mr. O'Doyle didn't create Mr. Flux, does that mean it was . . . Petey?"

"I think so. This picture is probably close to, if not the exact moment, it happened. That's why Mr. Flux didn't want the Clock Watchers near these books."

"We need Petey, don't we?"

"Fast."

"Can you pedal this time?" Sheed asked, righting the bike. He coughed into his fist. "All that dust got me feeling funny."

Sheed *looked* funny somehow. Like the time they'd played basketball all day and didn't drink any water, then had to lie in their beds the whole next day with Grandma placing ice packs on their foreheads and making them drink too much water. "Y'all mess around and give yourselves heat stroke," she'd said.

Today, as long as it had been, wasn't that hot, though.

Otto's throat was dry, so maybe some water would help.

They'd get some at the hardware store, then they'd get Petey so they could fix this mess.

Otto allowed Sheed to hop on the handlebars, and he got them going.

Sheed was grateful. He'd need his energy for whatever came next.

22

The Disappearing Downer

COMPLETELY GASSED FROM THE FAST ride to Archie's, Otto immediately went to the cooler near the door, unfroze two bottles of water, and handed one to Sheed. They were happy to discover their unfreezing ability worked perfectly on the liquid and gulped greedily until the bottles were empty.

"Mr. Archie"—Otto went for another couple of bottles—"could you add four waters to our tab?"

"Sure thing, fellas. Any luck on unsticking everything?"

"Actually, we think we found a big clue to solving the problem. It's why we're back. We need Petey."

Anna Archie said, "Oh, really? Petey can help save the day! See, Petey? It's like I always tell you—you're destined for big things."

Everyone waited for the inevitable and predictable

response. Something sad, a downer. Petey having absolutely no confidence in himself or what he could do.

They waited. And waited.

Sheed said, "Hey, Petey? Did you hear Anna say something nice you can contradict?"

Still, Petey didn't answer.

The boys rushed to the back of the store, where Petey had been during their earlier shopping spree. Only his broom and apron remained. The dour clerk was gone.

"Mr. Archie," Otto said, "Anna, do you have any idea what happened to Petey?"

"No," they answered.

Mr. Archie said, "I thought he'd gone mighty quiet, but figured maybe he'd dozed off."

"Dad, that's because you dozed off. I heard you snoring."

Mr. Archie laughed a laugh that might have been accompanied by a thigh slap had he been mobile. "You got me there, honey."

Anna said, "I don't know where he could've gotten off to."

Sheed searched the aisles, on guard, knowing today of all days, anything could happen. "Anna, no one came in here? No stranger in a black suit and a tall hat?"

"Nope. No suit and hat."

Otto said, "Anybody with dreadlocks and weird not-from-here clothes?"

"Uh-unh. I like weird clothes, so I would've noticed that."

No sign of Mr. Flux or TimeStar. The boys didn't ask about the Clock Watchers. If the Archies knew anything, they would've told. Given how fast A.M. and P.M. moved, it was possible they, or someone like them, might've discovered the same yearbook photos they had and zipped Petey out of there faster than Mr. Archie or Anna would've noticed. That had to be it, since Petey was stuck in time like everyone else. There was no way of knowing where they might've taken him, so add Disappearing Petey to the list of mysteries needing solving.

"Can you give us Petey's address?" Otto asked. If they couldn't find him, maybe there'd be better clues where he lived.

Mr. Archie said, "He stays with his mama at 2814 Thompson Street."

"Thank you!" said Sheed. "We'll get this all sorted as soon as we can."

Another bike ride took them over to Thompson Street, where all the houses were nearly identical. They were shaped the same—cottages with small square lawns. All painted pastel, alternating between blue, pink, green, and yellow. All the grass was the same length. No one had fences. There were no sidewalks, only wide, flat shale steppingstones arranged in the same curving path from the pale concrete driveways to the whitewashed porch steps. Otto had the creepy sensation that, on a normal day, they could've knocked on any door and met a version of Petey and Petey's mom.

Sheed had a similar creepy thought: that all of the doors would open at once and multiple Peteys would step onto multiple porches, waving at them in unison.

They shuddered, pushed such visions from their minds. Starting down the hill to search for the one true Petey, Sheed grabbed Otto's shirttail, whispered, "TimeStar."

The man who claimed to be a superhero time traveler emerged from between two houses, across the street from Petey's place. There was no gyrating sack on his shoulder, so he hadn't recaptured Witching Hour like he'd said he would. Nor did he seem very concerned with that particular mission. He strolled right up to 2814, Petey's house, and let himself in.

Only then did the boys notice the basement windows of that house glowing with electric blue light.

"What do you think is going on there?" Sheed asked.

"I know how we can find out. Maneuver #14?"

Sheed grinned. "Sweet. I could use the practice."

Leaving the bike at the corner, they moved stealthily down to 2814 Thompson and crept to a side door. Fishing in a pocket on Otto's backpack, Sheed pulled free a small plastic case, took a minute to poof his 'fro as he always did before delving into deep concentration, then revealed his trusty lock picks.

With his tongue poked between his teeth and one eyebrow cocked, he flexed his fingers like an artist set to paint a masterpiece, then went to work on the lock, sliding the slim tools in and out of the keyhole. He turned, and twisted, and jiggled. Otto watched the yard—for what, he wasn't sure —but the maneuver called for a lookout, so he looked out.

Another twist, another turn, then a click. "Got it."

Sheed nudged the back door open. They snuck inside.

The side entrance put them into a laundry room, which didn't seem very different from Grandma's laundry room except for a tiny detail. The washer and dryer looked homemade.

There wasn't the smooth exterior with a familiar appliance company name, no sir. These were made of welded and riveted metal. The control panels were pieced-together displays and switches that seemed to come from a dozen sources. Sheed glanced behind the machine, didn't see any sort of pipes for water or power cords for electricity. "It looks like something Leen Ellison would build."

"Not unless this washer and dryer can come to life and try to step on us."

For several seconds they eyed the appliances warily.

Otto nudged Sheed forward. They crept into the kitchen and found everything in there pieced together, too. The fridge seemed to be made out of car parts, while the oven seemed a mix of wrought-iron fencing and safety glass.

Sheed eyed Otto; Otto shrugged. He didn't know what to make of it either.

He was more concerned about running into Petey's mother, who might alert TimeStar to their presence with a yell. A quick search put that fear to rest. This level of the house was empty.

The basement below them was not.

The thudding and rustling were loud enough to be heard through the floor. The door leading down there was just off the kitchen. That incredible blue light leaked from beneath it.

Out of options and patience, they nodded in silent agreement, then burst into the basement. They landed at the bottom of the stairs, fists clenched and in fighting stances. "What are you up to, TimeStar?"

The time traveler, who'd been sitting on a workbench looking distraught, sprang to his feet and said, "Fellas, what are you doing here?"

Otto said, "I should ask you the same—"

He lost his words when he saw who stood next to Time-Star. Petey, somehow unstuck and frowny as usual, said, "Oh heck. More guests, and me with no snacks. Can this day get any worse?"

23
Not a Mannequin Challenge

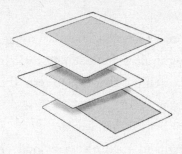

SHEED SAID, "WE'RE NOT WORRIED about snacks, Petey."

"I'm a little hungry," Otto said.

Sheed ignored Otto and, in an uncharacteristic show of emotion, threw himself at Petey, embracing him. "Good to see you moving."

Otto said, "*How* are you moving?"

Not only that, why was he wearing a white lab coat, like scientists wore on TV?

The answers Otto deduced from the strange cluttered basement. One wall was crowded with tacked-up plans and schematics; another was piled high with tinkerer junk; the bench TimeStar occupied was littered with snipped wires, and tools, and computer equipment. As Sheed mentioned upstairs, they'd seen sights like this before in Leen Ellison's mad science workshop.

"Petey." Otto tried hard not to let his surprise and confusion come off as insulting. "You're *a genius*?"

Eyes low, no confidence, Petey shrugged. "Not really."

He tossed aside what looked like a power screwdriver only it didn't hit the ground. It wasn't time stuck like they'd grown accustomed to. No, this tool sprouted propellers the moment it left Petey's hand and hovered to a designated spot on a nearby rack.

Petey said, "Wire cutters, to me."

From that same tool rack, a pair of yellow-handled wire cutters hovered on their own propellers, floated just above Petey's waiting palm, and dropped into his hand. He turned his attention back to some project the boys could not see.

Sheed shouted, revving up a tantrum. "This is all so much weirder than our usual Logan messes. Somebody better explain stuff to us, or . . . OR . . ." He grabbed what looked like a fire extinguisher and aimed the nozzle at Petey. "I'm going to lose it and foam this whole place up."

TimeStar tilted his head, watching Sheed's growing rage with . . . amusement?

Petey only spared him the mildest of glances. "I don't suggest you do that. That's not a fire extinguisher. It's a highly unstable explosive gel."

Sheed quickly, and gently, placed the canister on the ground. "You make explosives here?"

"No," said Petey, "it really was a fire extinguisher. I just wanted you to put it down."

TimeStar laughed. "Nice joke, Petey."

Petey said. "It could've been better."

All of this was overwhelming. And this was a couple of boys who'd faced laughing locust swarms, ghosts, and were-bears—just in June! It took a lot to overwhelm them.

Sheed pointed at TimeStar. "What are *you* doing here?" Then he pointed at Petey. "What are you *doing* here?"

Petey, still fiddling, spoke with his back to them. "You should pick your questions more wisely. If you're precise, then I can disappoint you precisely. I'm sure I won't have answers you like."

Otto said, "Start with how you got unfrozen. If you did it, maybe we can help other people get unstuck."

"Negative," said Petey.

Was he speaking of his general disposition or dismissing Otto's logic?

Petey elaborated. "I can't help other people get unstuck because I was never stuck."

Sheed said, "Sure you were. We saw you frozen at the hardware store like Mr. Archie and Anna."

"No. I was there, but only pretending to be frozen."

"Why?" Otto and Sheed said together.

"Because when Mr. A and Anna did it, I thought it was a thing. Like a mannequin challenge. I didn't want to mess it up."

That required a moment of reflection.

"When you saw us," Otto, wondering if Petey might be insane, said, "why didn't you stop then?"

"I didn't want anyone to know I'd been pretending. I didn't want anyone mad at me. That always sucks."

TimeStar spoke up. "Petey, it's like I've been trying to tell you, you're too hard on yourself. You worry too much about what other people think."

"Easy for you to say. You've traversed time and space.

Where you come from, I bet everyone thinks good stuff about you."

TimeStar flicked his eyes at the boys, changed the subject. "Well, why don't we help Otto and Sheed the best way we can so you and I can get back to our *confidential* business?"

Petey slumped, looking more defeated than usual. "We don't have any business, sir. I took a look at that device you brought me—"

TimeStar leapt to Petey's side, attempting to cut him off. "We don't have to discuss the details."

"But I already told you there's no way I can fix it. It's too advanced. I don't understand one thing about it."

TimeStar's face flattened; his brow became shadowy and frustrated. "I thought we were clear on the 'confidential' part of that conversation."

Petey said, "Otto and Sheed won't tell your secret. Will you, guys?"

"We don't *know* his secret," Sheed said. "Dude, why are you *really* here? It seems mighty convenient that a vacationing, time-traveling superhero accidentally shows up in Logan the same day time freezes. Ain't that right, Otto?"

"My cousin makes a valid point, TimeStar. There's a ton of weirdness in Logan County, but few coincidences."

"Fellas," TimeStar began, then he juked left, grabbing

his device from Petey and bolting for the door. Otto and Sheed were prepared for this.

Otto threw himself in TimeStar's path, curling up like a pillbug. When TimeStar skidded to a stop, Sheed shoved him so he tripped over Otto and sprawled on the basement floor. The boys scrambled, sat on him.

He groaned beneath their weight, but didn't struggle otherwise. "Maneuver #19? Really, guys?"

Otto snatched the device from TimeStar's hand.

"Be careful," TimeStar warned.

It was like metal, but *not* metal, not any kind Otto had ever seen. It was smooth, pentagonal, with three display windows that all blinked with numbers. Beneath the displays were embedded buttons. One side was a curved groove that Otto's thumb slid into naturally for a better grip.

"What is this, Petey?" Otto asked.

"He says it's what allows him to time travel. But it's broken. He can't go home."

Sheed bounced on TimeStar's back, making him *oof!* "You weren't planning to leave until *after* you helped us, right, *hero?*"

"Get off me, Sheed!" TimeStar yelled. "You too, Otto. I'll explain what I can."

The boys exchanged glances, came to a silent agreement, then let him up. Making sure to position themselves between him and the stairs. Otto kept a tight grip on his precious time travel device.

TimeStar rose, wincing, rotating his right shoulder so it made cracking sounds. "You two are heavy."

"Explain," Sheed said.

"I messed up. I'm not supposed to be here. I may have made this day worse." He flopped on Petey's workbench. "I may have made it so it can't be fixed."

It was not the explanation Otto and Sheed were hoping for.

24
The Big Key

"AS I TOLD YOU," TIMESTAR CONTINUED, "in the
future we all know about your adventures. You inspire us."

"Us?" Sheed said. "Like, other heroes?"

TimeStar's gaze softened. "Yeah, Sheed. You especially."

Otto bristled. Why *him* especially? "Keep going."

"I maybe didn't tell you the whole truth, okay. It's not
exactly legal for me to take this trip back to Logan. I
shouldn't be here. At all."

Otto snatched his pad from his pocket, scribbled furiously, underlining key points.

ENTRY #72

Not telling _whole_ truth

Illegal trip "back to Logan"

Shouldn't be here at all

"What else aren't you telling us, TimeStar?" Otto didn't sense any malice from the man. But his story still didn't seem . . . complete?

Otto wondered if Sheed felt the same way, but suspected TimeStar had won him over with that "you especially" silliness. Otto circled that part and added a question.

ENTRY #73
"Yeah, Sheed. You especially."

Biggest lie of all? LIKELY!

Sheed said, "Otto, you're usually the one that deals with all the far-out stuff. If TimeStar says we're all that in the future, and people worship us—"

TimeStar interjected. "I said 'were inspired by.'"

"Close enough. What are we worried about, then? That means everything turns out okay."

Shadows grew across TimeStar's face. "No. That's not what it means. According to the historical records, this was supposed to be one of your easier adventures. You two stopped Mr. Flux back on Harkness Hill almost immediately. You barely got your hands dirty."

"How?" Otto asked.

"He was going to use the camera on you. Freeze the both of you the same way you froze Fry. But, when he backed up to get the best shot, he tripped over a root, rolled down the hill with the camera. In the fall, the shutter got triggered with the camera angled at him, and he froze himself mid-tumble. He wouldn't tell you anything, but you went looking for help and came across A.M. and P.M, who led you to the other Clock Watchers, who eventually led you to Witching Hour. That's how I knew to find her. Once she explained everything to you, you went back to Flux and tricked him into unfreezing himself, which unfroze everything else. But none of that ever happened because—"

"You appeared and prevented him from falling," said Otto.

TimeStar's face sagged. "The reason these sorts of trips are outlawed by the Time Bureau is because people from the future should never change things about the past." He nodded at Otto's pad. "It's important that you know that."

"Oh." Otto said, and scribbled:

ENTRY #74
You shouldn't change things about the
past.

TimeStar said, "As you see, me dropping in the way I did changed things."

Sheed bounced on his toes. "You should've told us

sooner. Sure, you changed what was supposed to happen, but now we know how to stop him. If we take his picture and freeze him, he'll have to reverse the whole thing."

Otto reviewed his notes, bothered by something . . . some deduction . . . that eluded him. Still, Sheed made a good point. "Yes, it stands to reason that the same tactic should work."

TimeStar shook his head. "It's possible, but unlikely that you'll get your shot. Remember, in the original timeline, he took his own picture accidentally. How can you duplicate such a random event? He sure won't pose for you willingly."

"Thanks for those encouraging words," said Sheed. "It's really cool how you messed everything up, then tried to run back to your time."

TimeStar said, "I thought if I got out of the way, you two would figure this out on your own. I was never supposed to interfere, so the longer I'm here, the more things I might change."

Otto, still puzzling over the day's notes, said, "Why come to Petey?"

"He doesn't believe it, and you may not either, but Petey's one of the best inventors on the planet. When it comes to brilliant technical minds in Logan County, it's him or Evangeleen Ellison, right?"

Otto took note of that, too — at least he didn't say *Wiki*, ugh!

But Petey? One of earth's most inventive minds? Petey?!

Sheed said, "Petey, why aren't you frozen?"

He shrugged. "I suspect it has something to do with this." Petey unbuttoned his shirt and revealed some kind of glowing, heavily wired chest plate.

"What is that?" Otto was suddenly worried their friend and longtime hardware clerk was a cyborg.

"It's for my allergies." Petey buttoned his shirt again. "None of the nasal sprays or pills my doctor gave me were effective. So I built a temporal field generator that covers my entire body and shifts all allergens I come in contact with—mold, pollen, ragweed—two seconds into my past. I haven't sneezed since I turned it on back in the spring. This whole basement's outfitted with a similar technology. My theory is it makes me and everything in this room immune to time anomalies."

Okay.

"That's what I'm talking about, Petey." TimeStar gripped the genius's shoulders. "You can send your sneezes into the past. You do know something about time travel."

Bashful, Petey didn't bother denying the things Time-Star said he was capable of. He simply pulled away and sat in the corner.

Otto flipped back to previous notes, to Mr. Flux's mention of Peter. "I don't know about time travel, or your inventions, but I do know you're connected to Mr. Flux somehow.

Witching Hour told us he was created in a terrible moment of Missed Opportunity. I think that moment had something to do with Donny O'Doyle and the Lincoln play from when you were in high school. Do you remember it?"

Otto retrieved the yearbook from his backpack and showed Petey the old drama club photo.

"How do you know about that?" Petey's cheeks blazed, and he turned to his workbench, sniffling, not from allergies. "You're the Legendary Alston Boys—of course you found out about that stupid play. That's when I learned my place, fellas. Please leave me alone."

Sheed joined Otto. "Petey, we could really use you right now. You'd be helping us out, like at the hardware store."

Petey didn't budge, so the boys went over to him. As they stood to either side of him, they spotted the wallet-size photo of a beaming Anna Archie pinned to a board above his workspace. Otto nudged Sheed and pointed.

Sheed smirked. Petey liked Anna. Who knew?

Holding up his palm, Sheed gave Otto the signal to back off while he tried a new tactic.

"Petey," Sheed said. "You know we do the save-Logan-County-thing a lot."

"Sure. You guys are great!"

"Thanks. But, this is way over our heads. If you helped us, and we fixed this time freeze mess, we couldn't take all the credit. We'd have to tell Mayor Ahmed. He'd have to tell the guy who makes Keys to the City. That guy might have to—" Sheed snapped his fingers, as if a new thought popped into his head. "Otto, where do they get the metal to make Keys to the City?"

"Mr. Archie."

Petey nodded. "I remember helping with the order the last time that happened. I did the engraving. It was a key for the Ellison girls."

Otto scowled. "How big was it?"

Sheed slugged him in the shoulder. "However big it was, the key they make for this adventure is bound to be the biggest of all. It would have to be to fit all three of our names on it."

Petey perked up. "Three names?"

"If you help us, your name goes on the key, too. You couldn't engrave it yourself, though. It's bad luck. Who else at the store does engravings?"

"Anna." Petey's voice was light and dreamy. "She's great at engraving. She's great at everything."

That might have been the first positive thing they'd ever heard him say.

"There you go. If you help us, when we get the Key to the City, Anna can engrave all of our names on it. Heck, yours might be the biggest name she engraves. You could even keep the key here in your workshop."

"I don't know about all that," Otto said.

Sheed punched him again. The key was less important than the recognition—or rather, who would be recognizing Petey. As observant as Otto was, how did he not see the total crush Petey had on Anna Archie? How much other obvious stuff had he missed?

Sheed's fast talk pulled the dour clerk to their side. Petey left his bench and tore one of his strange schematics off the corkboard wall. "If you guys want to take a picture of that Mr. Flux, I think I have a way to make him stand still."

Otto, Sheed, and TimeStar gathered around, eyeing Petey's design.

"What is it?" Otto asked.

Petey said, "You ever hear of flypaper?"

Everyone nodded.

"So imagine the fly is *really* big."

25
Beware of Garden Pests

SHEED HAD BEEN WORRIED ABOUT whether a human trap would work on someone who wasn't human, so he was really enthusiastic about Petey's Giant Flypaper. Regular flypaper was sticky and smelled like things flies liked, so they got drawn to it. Petey's design wasn't exactly that. He didn't know what Mr. Flux liked to smell.

"Cinnamon buns," Petey said, "are something everyone likes smelling. My trap isn't based on smell, but I'm going to add Cinnamon Bun scent just to be safe."

"Do what you think is best," said Sheed.

While smell was not the primary bait, Petey's workshop became much more pleasant when it smelled like dessert. The actual bait wasn't based in smell at all. "It's going to be that camera."

Otto clutched it protectively when Petey pointed.

TimeStar said, "You want to use that thing as bait?

What if the trap goes wrong and Flux actually gets it? There would be no hope."

Petey got frowny and like his normal self again, abandoned his design on the worktable. "You're right. It won't work. Sorry, guys."

"No!" Otto and Sheed shouted, giving TimeStar dirty looks.

"It's a great plan," Otto said.

"Really sweet! And I'm not talking about the cinnamon bun smell."

Now Otto wished TimeStar had figured a way to go home. His meddling was making things harder. Scrambling to save the plan—and Petey's confidence—Otto said, "What if we pretended the camera was bait?"

"How so?"

"We make something that looks like the camera. I take it, and *I* become the bait."

Sheed said, "Otto, naw."

Yes. This was perfect. Also, it was a good way to get his name first and biggest on their next Key to the City. Take that, Wiki! "Mr. Flux has already seen me with the camera, so it won't seem strange when I'm the one luring him into the trap. Sheed, you can hold on to the real camera and hide out with Petey and TimeStar."

Sheed shook his head. "If something goes wrong, Mr. Flux will have you."

"Petey's plan is solid. Nothing will go wrong. Right?"

Sheed, reluctant but understanding the need to preserve Petey's confidence, said, "Right."

Otto scowled at TimeStar. "Right?"

"Right," said TimeStar.

Otto said, "Great. Petey, tell us how we set this trap."

"This particular design will only work in one place. My ma's garden." He snapped his fingers several times, pointed at various wooden crates around the workshop. "Grab those boxes, and let's go outside to set up."

Everyone did as told, grabbing boxes that were big but surprisingly light. Otto could've thrown his like a football. Sheed looked like a circus strongman lifting his one-handed.

TimeStar said, "These boxes should weigh more, shouldn't they? The size alone."

Petey held a bag open, whistled, and his drone tools hovered from their racked positions into the sack. "I'm usually here by myself. With no help, I had to find a way to move heavy items on my own. Those boxes are equipped with gravity dampeners I activated when I snapped my fingers. They make whatever I put in them nearly weightless."

Otto's jaw dropped. Every single one of Petey's inventions seemed like something out of the wildest sci-fi comics and movies. The kind of stuff that turned inventors into gazillionaires. And he was keeping it all to himself here in this basement.

Though, Otto supposed, the flip side was some-one like Leen Ellison, who failed to keep her inventions contained anywhere, usually resulting in mayhem. Maybe Petey was being extremely responsible, though Otto's deductive mind considered that unlikely. Whatever Petey's missed opportunity was, it had to have something to do with all these far-out gadgets and his lack of confidence.

Otto copied Sheed's one-handed grip on his own bulky box, took it a step further, balancing the crate on one finger. "This is awesome, Petey."

"Thanks. Be sure not to hold those boxes over your head, though. The dampener technology is glitchy, so you don't want a fully weighted box falling on you if there's suddenly an outage. They weigh about a thousand pounds each. Let's go to the garden."

Petey led the way, and everyone followed with their crates now held at arm's length. As fantastic as the technology was, no one wanted to be crushed like a bug if it went haywire.

Petey's backyard didn't have any of the eerie sameness the front of this neighborhood's homes displayed. While the yard on the immediate left contained a pink bucket-like aboveground pool and the house to the right boasted a trampoline, Petey's yard was dense with foliage. Thick hedges created a rectangular perimeter along the property line. Inside the hedge wall was a single apple tree, a colorful flower garden with a huge, ragged hole in its center, tilled rows of growing vegetables—stumpy green zucchinis, bright yellow squash, and a patch of neatly trimmed grass, where they began setting the trap.

Petey's time-stuck mother was there, too, gripping a garden hose with a suspended spray of water misting over her flowers.

"Hey, Ma," Petey said, unpacking equipment.

"Hey, Lovebug," she said. "You've brought friends over. It's the first time in, oh, ever."

"This is Otto, Sheed, and TimeStar. I'm helping them fix whatever's going on today."

"You're so helpful, Bug."

Everyone greeted Petey's mom with a "hi, Missus Thunkle," then unpacked crates at Petey's direction. Before long, they had big patches of metallic sheets—the "fly-paper"—unspooled and placed at various points throughout the yard. Once those were laid, Petey ran cables from the sheets back to the house, connecting them all to a small generator.

"These become sticky when I turn the power on. When I turn them off, whatever's trapped is free," Petey explained.

Otto worked at concealing the power cables in the grass and dirt. "What made you build big flytraps?"

He chuckled. "I suppose that was a faulty comparison. It's not for flies. It's for mutant moles."

Otto, Sheed, and TimeStar stopped concealing cables, startled.

Otto said, "Did you say mutant *moles?*"

Pointing at the hole—roughly the size of a truck tire—in his mother's flower garden, Petey said, "Yep."

Sheed said, "Otto . . ."

His pad was out and open. "Already writing it down."

With the traps laid, Petey approached Otto, stared at the camera a moment. He produced some new device from his pocket. Small, cylindrical. He pointed, clicked a button, and several laser beams shot from the device, tracing over the camera. The device cut off abruptly. Petey said, "Be right back."

He disappeared into the basement. TimeStar approached the boys, sticking particularly close to Sheed. "Hey, that was pretty clever how you convinced Petey to help. You've always been a quick thinker," TimeStar said, then added, "according to historians."

Sheed grinned. "I guess I did sort of wing that. I'm glad it turned out okay."

Otto sighed. If TimeStar really was from the future, and really was a fan, then it was clear which Legendary

Alston Boy was *his* favorite. Sheed's head was going to get so big from this. After they finished with Flux, they'd have to make sending TimeStar back to whenever he came from a priority if Sheed was ever going to fit through a doorway again.

Petey emerged holding another camera that looked identical to the one that had caused all their problems.

Sheed took it, turned it over in his hands, showed it to his number one fan. TimeStar admired it, too.

"How?" Sheed asked.

"That's just your basic 3-D printing technology. Typically something that detailed would take hours, but my printer design works in a fraction of the time. This copy can even produce a flash when you press the shutter release, though no actual photos."

There were a few more moments of marveling before Otto interrupted all the awe. "Trap's set. We've got our fake camera. How do we get Mr. Flux here?"

TimeStar stepped forward, fished something from his jacket. "Leave that to me."

What he produced looked like the pistol their PE teacher used to start races on field day, but with dials on the side.

TimeStar said, "Basic flare gun. Well, basic in the future." He twisted the dials. "The default setting is typically 'help,' but you can customize as the situation allows."

After the final dial twist, he fired a brilliant red flare

into the sky. It shot hundreds of feet in the air, as bright and beautiful as Fourth of July fireworks. Somewhere short of the clouds, it exploded into four red letters that sizzled the daytime sky.

FLUX.

TimeStar said, "Places, everyone. It won't be long now."

26
The Bad Times

IT WAS LONG. AGONIZINGLY SO.

Otto caught a charley horse from standing in one spot with the fake camera and had to hop on one leg. Sheed dozed in the bushes next to Petey, whose confidence waned with every passing—or nonpassing—second. TimeStar stared at the last letter in his futuristic FLUX flare fizzling out completely, leaving unmarred sky and unmoving clouds behind.

Tired of being unused bait, Otto said, "I don't think he's coming, guys. Petey, cut off the fly/mole paper. "

Sheed jerked awake, the real time-freezing camera dangling around his neck. "Huh—wha?"

Petey flipped the switch on his control panel, and there was a crackle of static electricity in the air as the trap powered down. "This probably would've worked if I wasn't involved."

"Nonsense, Bug," said Missus Thunkle.

"I agree with your mom," a groggy Sheed said, pushing out of the hedges.

TimeStar left his hiding place in the shadowy basement doorway and heaved a disappointed breath. "Maybe this was too obvious. If he suspects it's a trap, why would he come?"

A long, darkly clothed arm stretched from the basement and tapped TimeStar's shoulder. He gulped. "Guys."

Otto, Sheed, and Petey turned his way. They gulped, too.

Mr. Flux emerged from behind TimeStar's shoulder, peered at them all, and said, "The better question is if this was a trap, why would I come *alone?*"

Otto yelled, "Petey! The paper!"

Petey reactivated the traps surrounding Otto, charging the air with static electricity that raised the hairs on Otto's neck and arms.

TimeStar spun around, aiming a punch at Mr. Flux's nose. A hand caught that fist of fury an inch before it connected. It belonged to a very large, very grouchy-looking, very *sweaty* Clock Watcher. He grabbed TimeStar's belt and hefted him off the ground.

Mr. Flux said, "Crunch Time, remove this obstacle."

"Whoa, whoa, whoa!" TimeStar yelled as he was hurled directly onto a sheet of fly/mole paper. The trapped worked perfectly, cementing TimeStar's back to it. His arms and legs swiped at the air, like a turtle that couldn't turn over.

"Fellas," TimeStar said, "get out of here."

They tried. But all of their escape routes were quickly cut off by more Clock Watchers. All, apparently, on Mr. Flux's side. Boxed in, with nowhere to go, Sheed eyed the nearby antigravity crates they'd hauled Petey's equipment in. He grabbed one of the feather-light boxes and told Petey, "Snap your fingers when I tell you."

Sheed threw the near weightless crate toward a trio of approaching Clock Watchers. As it sailed over their heads, he shouted, "Now!"

Petey snapped his fingers, deactivating the gravity dampeners. The now-heavy crate crashed on Clock Watcher heads and shattered, knocking them into a splintery pile. Three down . . . a lot more to go. Several squads of Clock Watchers spilled into the yard.

Mr. Flux eyed the camera around Otto's neck and strolled toward him with purpose. He stepped squarely on a sheet of the paper, trapping one foot. He took a long stride with his free foot, and his anchored leg stretched in that rubbery way of his. Recognizing the trap that snagged him, Flux said, "Smart."

"Sheed!" Otto and TimeStar yelled at once, their voices perfectly harmonized, almost indistinguishable.

Sheed raised the camera, planting Mr. Flux squarely

in the viewfinder while the villain's attention was on Otto. Thumb on the shutter, he pressed—

—at the exact moment a child-size Clock Watcher in blue-and-yellow-striped pajamas, a matching floppy hat, and a teddy bear dangling from one hand threw herself at Mr. Flux, knocking him from Sheed's view. Instead of capturing Flux in the camera's flash, Sheed caught that Clock Watcher, who froze, still airborne in her tackling pose.

Mr. Flux told his brave soldier, "Thank you Bed Time! Your sacrifice will not be forgotten."

She yawned. "My time for you, sir!"

Mr. Flux turned his gaze on Sheed and the *real* camera. "I believe that's my property."

Sheed went for another shot, but the ground vibrated beneath his feet with such force, it knocked him off balance so he missed his chance. Thunderous footsteps grew louder behind him.

Otto saw it coming, shouted, "Look out! Platypus!"

Another Clock Watcher rode a humongous, raging Time Suck straight at Sheed and Petey.

Sheed went left, Petey right as the thing barreled into the yard. Its massive feet stomping toward the fly/mole paper, where TimeStar was still trapped. Those feet would crush him.

"Petey, deactivate the paper!" Otto yelled.

Petey powered down the traps. TimeStar rolled from the path of the beast just in time. Free.

But so was Mr. Flux, who taunted Otto with his freedom. "Good try. Just not good enough. Night Time!"

A Clock Watcher whose whole body seemed a shifty cosmos of dark skies, dark clouds, and stars, with a lopsided fingernail moon where most people had faces, raised its arms high and wide. Deep shadow and shade spilled forth from the Clock Watcher's palms, cresting over Petey's yard like a tidal wave.

Otto pressed his hands into the new night, trying to feel his way through the darkness, anticipating Mr. Flux clutching his neck at any second. The darkness was so deep, Otto couldn't see his hands, even though they were just a few inches away. Frightened more than he'd ever been, he worried that this darkness might never go away. "Sheed!"

As quickly as it had come, the new night disappeared. Like a flipped light switch, the day was back. The Clock Watchers were gone. So was Mr. Flux.

The false camera still dangled around Otto's neck. The real camera was nowhere in sight.

Neither was Sheed.

Mr. Flux had taken him, too.

27
Double Take

"SHEED!"

It couldn't be true. Sheed was hiding, or maybe stuck, or maybe tossed in the neighbor's pool. Otto sprinted over and climbed the plastic steps. The water remained time-frozen, undisturbed. "Sheed!"

TimeStar joined in, checking the other yard beneath the trampoline. "Sheed!"

The two of them yelled the missing boy's name over and over, their voices doubling in the strange harmony that made it impossible to tell them apart. Petey helped search, even going as far as to check the mutant mole hole in his mother's flower garden. Otto and TimeStar became frantic, their voices and phrases matching each other in ways that drew Petey's attention. He stared at them, squinting, their words blending as precisely as a well-rehearsed choir.

"Sheed . . ."

". . . where . . ."

". . . are . . ."

". . . you?"

Missus Thunkle broke the news none of them wanted to hear. "I'm sorry, boys. If he was here, he would've answered by now."

Of course she was right. Of course Sheed wasn't beneath a flowerpot, or in the storm gutters.

A horrible vision of his lanky cousin frozen in time terrorized Otto. Sheed's tiny 'fro fixed in a not-quite-perfect halo forever.

Otto's lip trembled, his eyes burned. He turned away from TimeStar and Petey, not wanting them to see him cry. As the tears brimmed, TimeStar said, "No! No! Not here. I'm not supposed to lose him here."

Otto turned to TimeStar again. "Huh?"

The time traveler pounded his fist on one of the remaining antigravity crates, seemingly forgetting Otto, Petey, and Missus Thunkle were even around.

"It doesn't happen like this. I can't have messed it up this bad," he mumbled.

Otto approached the man cautiously, worried about the panic he was in. "You're going to hurt your hand if you keep banging on the box like that."

TimeStar's eyes widened, as if surprised he wasn't alone. "I—I'm sorry. It's just, this day, it wasn't supposed to—"

Awkward and embarrassed, TimeStar slapped his right hand on the right side of his neck, just behind his ear. At the same moment, Otto did the exact same thing.

Petey said, "Oh my goodness!"

"What's wrong?" Otto and TimeStar said together, harmonizing once more.

Petey leapt up and down in place, pointing between them. "Oh, oh, oh!"

Otto couldn't understand what had Petey so riled up. Were they under attack again? He scanned the area for incoming Clock Watchers. TimeStar plucked his goggles from his face, revealing familiar brown eyes. His chest heaved, and his shoulders slumped, as if expecting something unpleasant.

Petey, swinging his pointer finger between them, gathered his words. "You're him. He's you."

Otto still didn't get it.

Petey said, "You're the same person! TimeStar is you, Otto. Grown up. From the future."

For once, there was not a bit of doubt in Petey's voice.

28
The Two of You

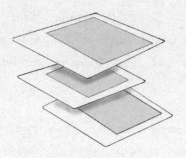

OTTO—A BOY WHO'D FACED monsters and ghosts, and who now lived in a frozen eternal day—understood there was Logan County strange, and then there was too strange. Too weird. Too CRAZY!

First of all, Otto would've noticed if he and Time-Star were *the same person*. How could he not? He had an extremely observant, deductive mind (despite what Wiki Ellison would have you believe). He'd jotted down notes after their rooftop conversation with TimeStar, recorded TimeStar's physical characteristics in great detail. Otto flipped his pad open, striking out prior summations and jotting new ones.

ENTRY #55
The stranger from the portal:

~~Has dreadlocks~~ Has stupid dreadlocks, like Sheed wants, not me.

~~Is skinny~~ Is TOO skinny. It's as if *donuts* don't exist in the future (preposterous) and I love donuts. So there.

~~Has a beard~~ Has an itchy-looking carpet on his face, and I would never, ever want that.

~~In his late 20s?~~ Is old as dirt and, just, NOPE!

DEDUCTION: ~~Inconclusive.~~ Petey is WRONG!

"Wrong. Wrong. Wrong." Otto said. "Right?"

Except . . . TimeStar wasn't saying wrong. He wasn't saying anything. Shouldn't he see how stupid this was and speak up?

With no word from TimeStar, Petey traveled down his usual path of self-doubt. "Or, maybe not."

Before Otto could agree, TimeStar said, "You're right, Petey. It's time to come clean."

"No," said Otto. "He's not right. I don't want to be clean. You aren't me."

"Ask me something only we would know."

"Don't say we."

"Just ask me something."

Otto was tempted to storm away. It was a foolish waste of time playing this game. They needed to find Sheed.

"Anything," TimeStar insisted. "At all."

Huffing, Otto said, "Fine. What grade did I get on the last math test of the year?"

"Oh, come on, Otto. That was a long time ago. It can't be that specific."

"That's where you're wrong. It was only three months ago. You said anything, and you failed. See, Petey? He's not me."

A patient TimeStar said, "Okay. I'll tell you something only we could know."

"Stop saying we."

"I know what happened that time Grandma's kitchen blew up in a ball of green fire."

Otto gulped. The official story was a gas leak. A green gas leak. The unofficial and true story involved a Bog Monster following him and Sheed home after they uncovered an eldritch patch of swamp deep in the Gnarled Forest.

"Even if you do know something other than what the fire chief put in his official report," Otto said, "you claimed all of our adventures were documented in the future. You could be getting the information from your historians."

"There are no historians. I made that up because there are rules to time travel, rules about what you can say or do because it can affect the future. I've made an illegal trip, but I still need to be careful. I didn't want you knowing all I'd lied about, so it wouldn't change *things* about the past." He stared intensely at Otto. "Do you understand?"

Otto shook his head, refusing to believe. He flipped to a page in his notepad. "You're from 2211. That's almost two hundred years from now."

"Otto, flip the numbers. Not 2211, but 1122. Sound familiar?"

It did. 1122. As in November 22.

Otto's birthday.

Wiki Ellison would've figure that out easy.

TimeStar said, "I'm really from twenty years in the future, Otto. Not two hundred. I'm you at the age of thirty-one."

"You're a liar!" Otto screamed, more mad than he'd ever been, not wanting to believe. "The bog monster, my birthday, could all be in your records. You don't know anything about me."

"When Witching Hour said the 'two of you' had secrets, she was talking about me and you, Otto. Get it?"

The two. Of you.

"You know my secret now, and I know yours," TimeStar said. "You're jealous of Sheed sometimes."

Otto's eyes burned.

"You think he's better at sports and more people like him. You're even jealous of Leen Ellison's crush on him because you don't think girls will ever like you. You think your Logan County fame and these adventures are all you have, so you chase them with everything in you."

TimeStar's voice sped up, deepened, almost like he wasn't talking to Otto, but some unseen audience. Someone important and far away. "You think without them you're a nobody, so you write down every little detail you can, and you read those notes at night with a flashlight when Sheed's snoring in his bed. They're better than comic books to you. Those Keys to the City from Mayor Ahmed are your prized possessions—you consider them yours, even though Sheed's name is on them too. Deep down, you tell yourself that you could've gotten them without his help, that you're the reason the Alston Boys are legendary." His intense gaze flicked away, and his voice softened. "You're wrong, though. About all of it. You'll come to regret all those thoughts. Guess you wouldn't know that part yet."

Petey stepped in then, grabbed TimeStar by the arm. "I think he gets it."

Tears streamed down Otto's cheeks. He sniveled, crying in a way that hadn't been acceptable since he was a real little kid. The embarrassing kind of crying. Ugly, snotting crying.

"You aren't me!" he shouted, and ran from the yard, wanting nothing else to do with TimeStar, or Petey, or Mr. Flux. It was all too much, and he was alone. Up the hill he ran, snatching Sheed's discarded bike, and he pedaled toward town with no particular destination in mind, half blind from searing tears. There was a horrid ache in his chest from TimeStar's sharp confession and his own keen deductions. Despite what he wanted to believe, he couldn't convince himself that the man wasn't telling the truth.

For all their differences in hair, and height, and weight, they shared the same eyes.

Otto swiped at his face, riding so fast that the tears he didn't mop away were seized by the breeze he created as he pushed the bike through the frozen Fry streets and past the stuck Fry citizens. Almost instinctively, he set a course for Butler Park. Specifically, the playground that used to be his and Sheed's favorite destination in all of Logan.

Through the open park gates he rode, shooting between the twisty slide and swing set. Little kids were frozen mid-stride between one fun apparatus and another.

A smoky scent hung in the air, along with an unmoving haze that had drifted from the open field where big kids sometimes played touch football, or tossed Frisbees. Otto slowed his pedaling.

Only a few people occupied the vast lawn. A couple

of picnic blankets were spread out beneath frozen families enjoying the perfect day. Off to the side, another familiar Fry resident was stuck in front of an oversize grill and a potbellied smoker. Mr. James, the local barbecue pit master, had brought all his equipment, coolers full of meat, and a big gallon jug of lava-colored hot sauce with the pump nozzle, ready for what would've been an epic cookout to close the summer.

On more than one occasion, Otto, Sheed, and Grandma had had the opportunity to enjoy hamburgers with the scorch lines; fat, just-burnt-enough hot dogs; sausages that squirted juice when you bit them; and Otto's favorite, sweet saucy ribs. All specialties of Mr. James. He always fed people until he ran out, and he never asked for money, though Fry residents were happy to pay him for such good food in spite of his resistance. He always said, "We look out for each other in Logan County. That's a bit of our strangeness I hope rubs off on the rest of this big, normal world."

All of Otto's Mr. James memories were good ones. He wanted to be reminded of good memories now, so he dropped his bike and gave in to the pull of the grill.

"Hey, Mr. James."

"Heyyyyy, Otto Alston. You can move!"

"Yeah, I didn't get stuck like everyone else." He glanced at the useless fake camera hanging against his chest. "You being stuck is kind of my fault."

"I have a hard time believing that. Even if that was the case, you weren't *trying* to make it so I couldn't move. Were you?"

"It's not just you, sir. It's all of Fry."

"Well. That is a mess. Still, you didn't mean it, did you?"

He was tired of not being honest. If TimeStar was really him, and he'd been lying to Otto all day, that made lying to himself truly distasteful now. "Maybe. I wanted summer to be longer."

"Everyone wants that!" Mr. James laughed through his unmoving lips. "Summer's the best time for cooking outside. The smells make everyone come and talk to me. I make people happiest in summer. There's nothing wrong with wanting that feeling to last."

"You still think that? Even being stuck at your grill?"

"Sure. Wanting something, and what you do about it, is two different things, young man. Knowing you and Sheed, I bet y'all doing all you can to fix it. Where is Sheed, by the way? I got them sausages he like."

Suddenly, talking to Mr. James, and being all honest, didn't feel so good. "I—I need to go find him."

"Don't let me hold you. I ain't going nowhere." A big belly laugh that time. "Tell you what, you two go on and get this day fixed, and once I can move again, I'mma make a plate for you, Sheed, and your grandma. Make sure you get some ribs. You dang near cleaned the bones last time!"

"Yes sir. I appreciate that, sir."

Otto turned away, bothered by something Mr. James had said. Something the reward of a big ole plate of ribs couldn't make him feel better about.

Where is Sheed, by the way?

Grabbing the bike, he put some distance between him and the delicious smells suspended around Mr. James's grill. He found a fairly isolated bench and sat down, consulted his notes, and scribbled some new thoughts.

ENTRY #76

TimeStar lied about a lot, but his lies made sense. If he told us too much, it might change things in the future. He said that's bad, and all the comics I read and movies I've seen agree.

QUESTION: Can I trust what he's saying now?

DEDUCTION: Maybe. There may be a definitive way to find out, thanks to, as much as I hate to admit it, Wiki Ellison (grrr).

Operating on the assumption that TimeStar was telling

the truth about his identity, and was indeed an older version
of Otto, brought up all sorts of questions about *why* he'd
traveled here in the first place.

ENTRY #77

TimeStar (it's just easier to keep
calling him that) claimed he wanted
to see me and Sheed take down the
Laughing Locusts.

QUESTION: Why would he need to see
what he already lived as me?

Otto chewed the end of his pencil, flipped to a previous
page in his pad, to the notes where TimeStar claimed his
time travel device was likely thrown off because of Logan
County weirdness. No, that wasn't exactly how he'd said it,
because Otto had placed the comment in quotes. TimeStar
had actually said because he came "back to Logan."

He began scribbling again.

DEDUCTION: At some point in the future,
I leave Logan.

QUESTION: Why?

Otto thought about this awhile. He'd probably go to

college. Maybe become a ship captain—that always seemed cool. Or a fighter pilot! *Maybe I fly futuristic jets that run on meteors or something!*

Otto's excitement faded quickly. There was no way to know for sure what TimeStar did in the future without asking. That mystery was the least of his concerns because . . . well . . . there was something TimeStar hadn't brought up, the thing Mr. James had asked about.

QUESTION: If TimeStar is really Old Me (and that seems more and more likely), then . . .

. . . where is *his* Sheed?

29
The Missing Sheed

SHEED DID NOT KNOW WHERE he was exactly.

He was jerked left, wrenched right, yanked up, and lurched down. It was like being stuck inside a rolling water balloon, but instead of actual water, the balloon was filled with a galaxy of stars, making him an astronaut with no suit. He held on to the camera he'd been entrusted with because there was nothing else to hang on to.

His stomach was not going to tolerate this ride much longer. Just when he thought a vomit comet was about to fly . . . he stopped moving.

No more bouncing, just stillness, settling his gut. The night balloon he'd been trapped inside popped like a soap bubble, and he landed on a hard floor surrounded by Clock Watchers. Among them, the black-suited Mr. Flux.

From the ground, the towering man seemed a million feet tall. Two million if you counted his hat. He bent at the

hip and stretched his spaghetti arms, his flattened dough hands, and his spider-leg fingers toward the camera. Sheed tried scooting away, but his path was blocked by the sweaty, dripping Clock Watcher who'd tossed TimeStar around back at Petey's.

"Crunch Time," Mr. Flux said, "give the boy some breathing room."

The sweaty hulk backed away, a light rain of perspiration pattering on the wooden floor.

As a disgusted Sheed avoided the puddle Crunch Time left behind, he barely felt Mr. Flux lift the camera strap from his neck. "Hey!"

Mr. Flux examined the device, which looked tiny and toylike in his ghoulishly stretched hands. His satisfied grin lengthened to a point where it might split his head in half as he peered through the viewfinder and pointed the camera at Sheed.

Sheed braced himself—or rather, tried to relax into a comfortable position he might be okay with should he be stuck in it for all eternity. The pose he settled on was something like a baseball player sliding into third base, but with his head propped on his elbow as if taking a nap. It was a pose he'd seen on Grandma's old R&B album covers. She said when singers posed like that, you knew they were feeling good about their music. Sheed wanted to feel good about being stuck forever, so it seemed like the right move.

He waited for the inevitable, time-freezing flash.

"Go on," Sheed said, sounding braver than he felt. "I ain't gonna beg you not to."

Mr. Flux lowered the camera. "I was hoping we could talk, actually."

Was this a trick? It had to be.

Surrounded, out of options, what choice did Sheed have but to play along? "Talk about what?"

"Walk with me, Rasheed."

He didn't move, fearing a sudden flash at the awkward moment he attempted to stand, and being stuck half bent over, staring at his shoelaces forever.

Mr. Flux said, "I promise if I'm going to freeze you, I'll allow you the opportunity to position yourself as you like. Hopefully, that won't be necessary. I'm all about opportunity, as you'll come to know. Please, walk."

Pushing himself off the ground, Sheed found himself among a gang of Clock Watchers rivaling the library gathering. A bunch of Second Guessers and Minute Men who'd obviously abandoned Father Time and switched sides, the person-shaped living galaxy Night Time, plus many, many, many more. They parted as Mr. Flux moved, creating a path in this cramped standing-room-only place. Wherever they were.

The floor was made of solid wooden planks, old and knotty. Dim light beamed through gaps in boarded-up windows. Above their heads the frozen wheels, barrels, hooks, flies, cams, gears, and all the other intricate parts of Fry's giant clock.

They were in the tower in Town Square.

"Ten-oh-four a.m.," Mr. Flux said, pointing at the gears overhead. "All those precise parts to tell the people of the town what time it is. Where they should be at said time. What they should be doing. Yet it doesn't really tell anything, does it?"

The Clock Watchers around them murmured, shifted uncomfortably.

"Oh, don't take that the wrong way," Mr. Flux told

the room. "I'm not diminishing your former roles. I'm just expressing to the young man that time itself is not what determines a human's actions. It's not time that tells a woman when to be at her office. Her boss may dictate the length of the workday; then she chooses whether to be early, late, or on schedule. Isn't that right, Business Hours?"

A group of Clock Watchers—half of them women, and half of them men—all in matching blue suits, raised brown leather briefcases in an affirmative salute.

Mr. Flux continued, "When a child is naughty and is sent to sit in a corner, who insists on the length of the punishment? Tell us, Time Out." He pointed to a pouting toddler-size Clock Watcher with pigtails. Her arms were crossed, and one leg tantrum stomped.

Time Out said, "The mean mommy or daddy."

"Exactly. Do you see, Rasheed? Yet another example of humans deciding what to do with time. With *opportunity!* How often do you think they make the right decisions?"

They'd walked to just beneath the clock face, where the outside light glowed honey gold through its translucent glass cover. From inside the tower, the Roman numerals were reversed; the huge bells responsible for hourly gongs were giant sleeping bats in the gloomy rafters above. Mr. Flux waited for an answer.

"I don't know," Sheed said honestly. It wasn't something he'd ever considered.

"Nor do I. I can tell you one human whose error caused me grave pain."

Sheed suspected he knew the human Mr. Flux spoke of.

"Petey Thunkle did not use his time wisely. Not a grave sin in itself. But, there was a single critical moment that changed everything. Would you care to hear about it?"

There was no choice here. This was one of those rhetorical things Otto liked so much. Sheed nodded, and settled in for . . .

30

The Terrible Tale of Peter Thunkle's Missed Opportunity

PETEY THUNKLE WANTED ONLY normal smarts, because then maybe he'd get only normal teased. But Petey had smarter smarts than the smartest students at Fry High. As a freshman, he quickly worked his way into the most advanced science and math classes the school offered, stunning every teacher at every turn. Particularly on project days, when Petey showed up with inventions of a mind-boggling variety. He gave chemistry teacher Mr. Golden a "Grade Sorter." A machine that scanned the room, identified each student and their current seat, then sorted graded papers into the proper order, preventing the teacher from the inefficient practice of zigzagging all over the place when he needed to return exams. Mr. Golden loved it, gushed about it in front of the whole room. "Now I can get y'all your D's and F's much faster."

No one laughed at that joke.

Still, Mr. Golden loved Petey. And if teachers loved Petey, students hated Petey. With the exception of the lovely and sweet Anna Archie, who'd been voted Nicest Person every year since kindergarten.

She said, "I think your Grade Sorter is an awesome idea! Besides, I get A's, so I'm happy to have my tests back faster."

As wonderful as Anna was, her kindness did little to soften Fry High's general treatment of Petey. By the time Mr. Golden finished lavishing him with praise, even the "nerds" were bullying Petey. Though no nerd could outdo master bully Donny O'Doyle.

(At this point, Mr. Flux stopped the story and passed a hand over his own face. "My stunning resemblance to that lowlife O'Doyle is but one result of Petey's curse, and perhaps the least of them. You shall see.")

Physical harm was not Donny's greatest skill. His verbal violations were heavyweight punches. His shouted slander, kung-fu kicks. His boorish barbs, poison blow darts. All bruising, breaking, and slowly killing Petey's spirit.

If Petey brought a new invention to school, Donny would say it was ripped off from the Home Shopping Network. Not true, of course, but it didn't have to be. If Donny caught wind of Petey acing another math test, he'd say Petey was only good in math because he smelled like dog crap and needed to calculate the range of his own stench.

Always getting picked on, always getting laughed at,

and all while fighting the natural doubts any person is prone to when trying to create—it wore Petey down.

The genius inventor didn't want to stand out anymore.

He wanted invisibility, to disappear. People didn't bully what they couldn't see. Near the end of freshman year, he had a chance.

Mr. Golden, still getting maximum usage from his beloved Grade Sorter, raved about the design to one of his former classmates, the director of a big city think tank in Richmond, Virginia. This particular think tank was the Turing Unified Research and Development Institute. On the teacher's recommendation, they were interested in having Petey take a coveted summer intern position.

Mr. Golden explained think tanks were groups of smart people who worked on solving the world's problems. "These positions are usually reserved for college students," he said, "but I showed them your designs and grades, and told them that I think you're a smart young man who can use this shot. They want to meet with you. It's the chance of a lifetime."

At this same time, the spring production of *Lincoln: The True Story of Honest Abe's Honesty* was well into rehearsals, with opening night looming. Good news because Petey's wonderfully innovative holographic set designs would be displayed for the whole town. Bad news because Donny

O'Doyle had somehow managed to be cast as Lincoln, so they saw each other every day, during school and after.

The teasing was bad, but whenever Donny got Petey with a good one, Petey touched the Turing Institute letter in his back pocket, knowing his interview was coming up. For the first time in his life, he was confident things would go his way.

Until the day he lost the letter.

It was the final dress rehearsal, and Donny had called him Pee-Pee Petey to get the other actors and crew members laughing and relaxed. When Petey reached for his lucky letter, it wasn't in his pocket. He searched between all of his holographic projectors mounted in the catwalks above the stage, and under auditorium seats, and in the bandstand. Found nothing. Only deep into the play's final act did he notice a white scrap of paper visible behind a flickering, holographic prop stove he'd been working on earlier.

Donny gave his final rousing monologue, right before the John Wilkes Booth character snuck up on him. Petey, unable to resist, stepped from behind the backdrop, hoping to snatch his letter unseen. Donny—supposedly assassinated by then—was peeking, and shouted, "Hey, what you doing, Pee-Pee?"

Donny's Lincoln returned from the dead, ran over, and snatched Petey's letter.

For once, Petey fought back, attempting to reclaim what was his. Donny held the letter out of reach as he read it.

"Wait!" Donny said, and the auditorium went quiet. "Did y'all know Petey has a meeting with a *think tank* on Saturday?"

Unsurprisingly, no one in the room seemed to grasp the significance. That didn't stop Donny. "Turing Unified Research and Development Institute. That sounds like a pretty big deal, Petey. Is it a big deal?"

"Why, yes," Petey said. "It is a big deal. The Turing Institute is one of the biggest think tanks in the country."

"Huge-huge?"

Petey, feeling proud, said, "Ridiculously huge."

Donny nodded, gently handed back Petey's letter, and said, "Good stuff, bro. Turing Unified Research and Development Institute. Tell me something, did you notice what the initials spell?"

(Sheed, familiar with acronyms because of the BTS-FOASTG on Grandma's calendar, considered Donny's question and . . . dannnnng . . . understood just how bad things were about to go for Petey. The acronym for the Turing Unified Research and Development Institute was . . .)

"TURD!" Donny shouted. "Everyone, Pee-Pee Petey is going to a huge TURD institute."

Donny hooked his elbow around Petey's neck, dragging

him to the edge of stage in a headlock, leading a chant of "Huge TURD! Huge TURD!"

Everyone in the auditorium joined in. Actor. Stagehand. Director.

The doors at the back of the auditorium opened, and the roving yearbook photographer roamed in, needing a picture of the drama club. Petey's humiliation hit a new peak when he recognized her.

It was Anna Archie.

The chants continued. "Huge TURD! Huge TURD!"

Sweet, kind Anna went to the director and pleaded with him to stop the teasing. He rolled his eyes and claimed they were all just having fun, but eventually asked the cast to give it a rest so they could take a picture.

Even as the drama club posed for their group photo, Donny maintained Petey's headlock. And Petey, not wanting to appear weak and abused in front of Anna, smiled as if he was in on the gag.

Anna aimed her camera and instructed the group. "On three, say 'cheese.' One, two, three . . ."

The entire drama club said, "Huge TURD!" as the flash exploded.

The photo of that moment was immortalized in the yearbook picture Otto and Sheed would discover many years later.

Mr. Flux, reaching the tale's end, said, "Petey never

went to that interview. He decided then and there that no way he'd be caught dead at TURD Institute. He missed the opportunity Mr. Golden had granted him."

With a reptilian sneer, Mr. Flux said, "That was the day I was born. Any questions?"

31
Questions. Lots of Them.

SHEED SAID, "YOU WERE BORN because Petey missed an opportunity? Shouldn't there be a bunch of Missed Opportunities, then? Like millions?

"I believe I am unique." He seemed to be bragging and defensive at the same time. "A one in a billion—no trillion—anomaly, born from the oddness that saturates your county."

"But there *could* be others?" Sheed pushed.

"I doubt that."

"You don't know for sure? What if you have brothers and sisters? Or cousins, like me and Otto?"

"I don't have cousins."

"You might, though."

"I do not!"

Sheed jerked at the snap in Mr. Flux's voice, but recovered quickly and moved on to his other questions. "Okay.

One time me and Otto were playing basketball at the park. I had the opportunity to hit the game winner, but I passed to Otto instead, and we lost. So I could have a Mr. Flux out there mad at me for not using my sweet crossover to win?"

"No."

"Okay. One time I missed an opportunity to stick Otto's hand in a bowl of warm water while he was sleeping. Since I didn't do that, there could be an Otto missed opportunity walking around with permanently wet sheets?"

"Enough!" Mr. Flux roared. "I didn't mean for you to actually ask questions. I thought you'd nod and look grim with understanding. My point was to tell you how I got here and why I'm doing what I'm doing. That's all. I'm not a missed opportunity tour guide."

"I still don't understand. Freezing time so no one else misses an opportunity, is that you being helpful or you being vengeful?"

Mr. Flux's jaw clenched; he was clearly flustered by Sheed's line of questioning.

Sheed continued, "Sorry. I'm just thinking if people miss opportunities all the time, why is yours so special that you gotta turn all bitter and villainous instead of just moving on like everyone else?"

Mr. Flux exploded, "Because I was trapped with these idiots!" He swept an arm toward the Clock Watchers, who looked hurt and offended, but kept quiet otherwise.

"Whatever strange magic infects this county you live in made my birth possible. But it also trapped me. I couldn't leave! Every time I tried to venture into the world beyond Logan, I'd hit an invisible wall at the county border."

Sheed said, "You were like a bird that flies into really clear glass?"

Flux scowled. "An apt analogy, Rasheed. Yes, I was a bird, trapped behind glass. Except humans can see birds, and help birds if they so choose. Humans couldn't see me because I was in the Clock Watcher dimension. No matter how much I screamed and begged."

A chill raised goose bumps on Sheed's arms, as the horror of what Mr. Flux described sank in. "You were alone like that for years. Like a ghost."

"Oh no." Mr. Flux shook his head with such extreme force it twisted his neck like a wet dishrag. "I wasn't totally alone. The Clock Watchers were there, also invisible to the human eye. Though most were too busy with their repetitive routines to concern themselves with me while I screamed myself mad. So many of them ignored me in my torment. Father Time. The Golden Hours. They had tasks way more important than a poor trapped soul like me. So, one day, I stopped screaming and started thinking. Observing. I began to understand that the Clock Watchers interacted with the human dimension all the time, but in slavish ways that reflected their unique natures. Maybe, just maybe, I could interact with the human world, too. And make everyone in this town pay for abandoning me. With the help of the right Clock Watcher. "

"That's when you found Witching Hour, and got her to build your camera and make it so we could see you," Sheed said, knowing the rest. "You tricked us into doing your dirty work."

"Ah, yes. Frozen time changes the rules in both dimensions. It means the residents of Fry can never let another opportunity slip by, and I can now roam freely without Witching Hour's aid." Mr. Flux applauded lightly. "You Alston Boys are so helpful."

"Why yap all this to me?"

Mr. Flux clasped his hands behind his back, pinched his lips together, took on a troubled posture. "It seems that I made a miscalculation. I did not think very far beyond my vengeance. With my goal achieved, what now? I have this camera, I could leave Logan County, but where would I go? What should I do?"

Sheed hadn't considered those questions. Now that they were in his head, the possible answers were quite frightening.

"I could go to more towns. Take more pictures. Prevent more people from missing opportunities. But that is lonely work, and I've been alone for far too long. Certainly, my loyal Clock Watchers are a useful army. Not very intellectually stimulating, though. Isn't that right, Quitting Time?"

A stout, grouchy Clock Watcher in a hardhat and a sleeveless flannel shirt, who carried an aluminum lunch pail, said, "I'm knocking off for the day!" Then she left.

Mr. Flux said, "She'll be back in a moment, then she'll do that again. Over and over. Do you see my problem?"

Sheed's lip curled, and an eyebrow arched. "You want me and Otto to work with you?"

"*For* me!" Mr. Flux clarified, waving one finger. "For me. Also, not you *and* Octavius. You."

Sheed did not know how to respond to that.

Mr. Flux said, "I told you I could see the people in this county when I was in my specter-like state. You were no exception. What I observed, well, it was downright criminal. Those adventures you two go on, *you're* the heart of your team, Rasheed. He's the brain—no offense to your smarts—I respect both. He does not. He's often rude to you. Dismissive. Haughty, even."

Sheed mumbled, "I don't know what *haughty* means."

"And I will never make you feel bad about that. Would Octavius?"

Sheed had never been embarrassed about not knowing stuff. That's what learning is for. Yet, he remembered times he'd made such a confession to Otto, and his cousin would sneer, and scoff, and say things like, "How do you *not* know that?" As if not having his brain was a crime.

"I've seen you under pressure, Rasheed. You're good in a

217

clutch. Instinct is your friend. That sort of leadership would be valuable in my new adventures. I have won. Even if you don't realize it yet, you will. This is your latest opportunity, Rasheed. Don't let it be your last." Mr. Flux crouched aimed the camera, and peered at Sheed through the viewfinder. "What do you think of my proposal?"

Sheed did not say yes. He did not say no, either. He thought long and hard.

What would it be like to not have Otto breathing down my neck from now on? Not have him acting like I don't know what I'm talking about, or that I'm only good for stuff like lifting his two-ton backpack? What would it be like to be something more than a Legendary Alston Boy?

That he couldn't outright dismiss Mr. Flux's "opportunity," in spite of the consequences for Fry, Logan County, and beyond, said a lot.

32
A Condo?

ON SHEED'S BIKE, INTENT ON getting back to Petey's as fast as his legs could manage, Otto made it only a few yards before a shiny flicker caught his eye. Coasting closer, he recognized familiar glistening footprints. They weren't fresh, and the nearest ones faded right before his eyes. Pumping the pedals, he pushed himself to keep up with the vanishing trail, all through downtown Fry, finally ending at the door of the Nice Dream Ice Cream shop.

Otto dropped the bike at the curb and pushed through the shop's door. The Clock Watchers sitting on stools, at tables, and in booths were sullen, hunched over bowls of ice cream. Chocolate, vanilla, strawberry, and other flavors smeared their mouths as they shoveled down spoonful after spoonful, not even bothering to acknowledge his presence. On two stools, with elbows propped on the countertop, were the Golden Hours, looking sad as sad could be, their bowls piled high with no fewer than eight unmelting scoops each.

"A.M.," Otto said, "P.M., what's going on here?"

Only A.M. glanced over. P.M. kept shoveling ice cream.

"Guys?" Otto pleaded.

"Mr. Flux has won," A.M. said.

P.M. spoke, though his words were distorted by the spoon in his mouth. "Our thibilings thave thoined that thonster."

Otto took a second to translate: *Our siblings have joined that monster.*

A.M. said, "That monster made an offer that many of our brethren couldn't refuse. Clock Watchers need something to do. When time is frozen, there aren't many options."

"You two aren't thinking of joining Mr. Flux, are you?"

"Goodness, no. Have you seen his suit? Not even our skills are enough to help that situation."

That was good to hear, though not quite good enough. Scanning the room, Otto saw only a fraction of the Clock Watchers that he'd first encountered at the library. More Clock Watchers had attacked them in Petey's backyard than were in the shop now. Though he did see old, wise Father Time in a corner booth next to a less-than-energetic Game Time. Father Time had toffee chips in his beard.

"The thay est losht!" said P.M., shoving ice cream into his mouth.

Otto shook his head. "No. The day is *not* lost."

"My brother is right," said A.M. She stared glumly at Otto, and even her bright yellow skirt seemed duller somehow.

What could Otto say? The truth was he felt the same way. Everything that could go wrong had. And who was to blame?

Me, Otto thought. He just couldn't figure out if he meant current him or TimeStar him. Either way, he could not give up the day. "I know you guys like to move around a lot, but can you promise that you'll keep all these Clock Watchers here until I get back?"

"Depends," said A.M. "What would we be waiting on?"

"A plan," Otto said.

P.M. shrugged. "As long as there's ice cream, we'll be here."

It wasn't the most enthusiastic answer, but Otto took it, rushing from the shop and grabbing the bike again.

By the time he reached Petey's, he was gasping, and it felt like his heart might pump out of his chest. The way the day had been going, he'd expected to find Petey's house deserted, forcing him into another search mission to find TimeStar. For once, his luck held, Petey and TimeStar were still in the basement workshop, discussing their own futile strategies, looking as depressed as the ice cream shop Clock Watchers.

"Otto!" Petey said, happy to see him. Then correcting himself, "Younger Otto."

TimeStar said, "I'm happy you came back. I was worried."

"Where's Sheed?" Otto asked.

TimeStar said, "We were just discussing that. We were going to question Bed Time, the frozen Clock Watcher in the backyard, to see if she could tell us."

"No," Otto corrected him, scared to go down this path, but needing to. "Not *my* Sheed. *Your* Sheed. If you're a time-traveling adventurer, where's your partner?"

"He's on a separate adventure right now." TimeStar's eyes flicked left, and he frowned.

The liar tick.

Otto stomped forward, jabbing his finger at TimeStar. "You're not telling the truth. You did a lying tick thing that Wiki Ellison told me about, and I can't figure why you'd lie about Future Sheed unless something bad happens to him. You better tell me where my cousin is right now." Otto screamed, "Tell me!"

TimeStar placed a gentle hand on his shoulder. "Let's talk outside."

Otto ran from the basement into the backyard and sat with his back against Missus Thunkle's biggest flowerpot, cupping his face in his hands and crying out his fear. He knew he would not get rid of it all. TimeStar emerged from the basement and sat close. Side by side, the two of him.

"You don't recognize the name TimeStar. Do you?" he asked.

Otto shook his head. "Should I?"

"A lot of things are fuzzy to me now, but I'm certain we're a few months from when you and Sheed think it up. TimeStar is a superhero in the made-up comic book world you two like to draw. Your version has cooler clothes than what I'm wearing, though."

"Your clothes look cool to me," Otto sniveled.

"That's because you don't live where I live." He seemed to think that over. "Yet."

"What happened to your Sheed?" Otto was finally ready to hear if his most recent and horrible deduction was true. "Did he . . . die?"

TimeStar took several long, hard breaths before answering, "Yes."

Otto began crying again. "How? Is it one of our adventures? Do we run into something we can't handle?"

"I'm not sure I should tell you anything more. I have to be careful not to change —"

"Things about the past! I know!" In an emotional explosion that was as surprising as any of today's weirdness, Otto hauled off and hit TimeStar — an *adult* — in the chest. Hard. Hard enough to hurt his hand. "Why do you keep saying that? Stop saying that!"

TimeStar winced but didn't try to defend himself. Otto

hit him again and again. Creating a hollow drumbeat with every strike.

"Why are you here if you can't help Sheed not die? What good are you?"

Otto pounded on TimeStar until he was tired and had to catch his breath.

TimeStar massaged the areas where he'd been struck but showed no anger. "Talk about beating myself up."

"Don't make jokes!"

"I'm sorry, man. It's not some Logan County monster, nothing like that. He's sick. Or he will be."

Otto sprang to his feet. "That's it? Then we'll tell Grandma, and she'll get a doctor to fix him before he gets bad."

TimeStar was shaking his head from the moment Otto got to his feet. "It's not that simple. Some illnesses doctors can't fix. And you're not telling Grandma anything." TimeStar had an edge in his voice then. "Not one word. She deserves to have the rest of her time thinking both her grandsons will be fine, Otto."

That hit like a bucket of cold water. "The rest of her time? Grandma dies, too?"

"Otto, of course. Eventually." TimeStar slapped a hand behind his right ear, slowly rose, and retreated into Missus Thunkle's garden. "I knew I shouldn't have told you anything."

Otto stomped after him. "Too late for that. So you might as well keep flapping those gums."

TimeStar spun back toward him, head cocked. *"Flapping those gums?* Dude, you sound so much like her . . ."

Her was Grandma. That was one of *her* favorite sayings. Thinking about *her* hurt now. It never had before.

"It's a sickness that's in his blood," TimeStar said. "His cells. There's no cure."

"There has to be."

"There isn't."

"Not even in your time? Where you come from?"

TimeStar shook his head. "Even if there was, there are just certain things you don't do. Rules you don't break without . . . *consequences.* You start messing with the laws of nature too much, you become like Mr. Flux, messing stuff up so bad there's no telling if it can ever go back to normal."

Otto was mad again. Moving between sadness and anger this fast and hard would give him whiplash, but he couldn't stop. "There's no such thing as normal in Logan County! How could you forget that?"

"You'd be surprised how much you forget when you grow up. Stuff that used to be an adventure becomes scary. You worry about getting hurt and not being able to go to work."

"Are you a soldier?" Otto recognized how hopeful he sounded. "Or a pilot?"

"No. I'm neither of those things. I'm not going to tell

225

you details, but I sit at a desk most of the day. I look at a monitor."

"That sounds boring."

"It is. Want to hear something more boring? I—we—have a condo."

Otto didn't know what to say about that. He returned to the more important topic. "Why did you come here? What's the point? Sneak around like a creeper, then disappear? All you did was mess stuff up, and you can't help Sheed. Why bother?"

"I just wanted to see him again. All right?"

"No. It's not! Because you're telling me I'm going to give up and then I become a boring desk slug without Grandma or Sheed. That's not the way it's supposed to happen. I'm supposed to be a legend, with my cousin. Not live in a condo. Not be . . . be . . . you!"

TimeStar wrapped his arms around Otto. At first Otto tried to wrench away—fighting, punching, kicking. TimeStar didn't let go. He held on to his kid self until Otto buried his face in the time traveler's chest and cried some more, no longer embarrassed.

Why should he be when grown-up him, who'd broken the laws of physics and the future to glimpse his beloved cousin one more time, was crying too?

33
Maneuver #73

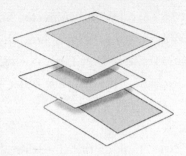

PETEY ALLOWED THEM THEIR MOMENT, though not a long one. He cleared his throat loudly, which made Otto and TimeStar separate. "I don't mean to interrupt, but we need to find that Mr. Flux guy, right?"

"Right." TimeStar turned away, fixing his face.

Otto did the same.

TimeStar pointed with his chin. "I bet she knows."

"She" was the Clock Watcher called Bed Time, still frozen from Sheed's camera shot. TimeStar puffed up his chest and made a show of cracking his knuckles, but when the childlike Clock Watcher's bottom lip began to quiver, he backed down. "Hey, hey, sorry. I didn't mean to scare you. It's just we need to know how to find Mr. Flux. I don't want things to get unpleasant between us, but—"

"He's in the clock tower," said Bed Time. "Him, a lot of Clock Watchers, and a bunch of Time Sucks."

"Really?" TimeStar sounded surprised. "That easy?"

"I don't like Mr. Flux. I want you to stop him."

Otto said, "Why were you helping him, then?"

"He said I could stay up." Bed Time yawned.

Awesome. Otto said, "Is there any other helpful stuff you can tell us?"

"You're going to lose."

Petey said, "I was thinking the same thing."

They'd been overwhelmed by Mr. Flux's backyard Clock Watcher attack. If the remaining Clock Watchers at the ice cream shop were the only ones who hadn't gone to his side, then Mr. Flux had a small army. Plus the camera. Plus Sheed.

Otto made himself not think much about his cousin, because he didn't want to cry again.

TimeStar said, "Any chance you've got a maneuver for this that I've forgotten about?"

"No. No maneuvers this ti—"

Hold on. That wasn't actually true.

Another of Grandma's favorite sayings was *you learn something new every day*. The Legendary Alston Boys' maneuvers always came from learning something new while on an adventure, something that Otto catalogued for later. There'd been a lot of new lessons today, one in particular just might be New Maneuver Worthy.

TimeStar said, "I know that look. What are you thinking, Otto?"

"I think we need to go for ice cream right now. Follow me."

So they did.

A.M. and P.M. still had full heaping bowls of creamy goodness when Otto, TimeStar, and Petey entered the Nice Dream Ice Cream shop. What had changed were the number of empty seats. There were fewer Clock Watchers here than before.

Otto said, "Did more of them go to Mr. Flux?"

Butter pecan dribbled down P.M.'s chin and dripped onto his neckerchief. "It would seem that way."

Otto's heart fell into his left shoe. They needed *more* support, not *less*. So many sullen faces here. Father Time simply bent forward, bumping his forehead on a table repeatedly. Game Time flicked glances at the door, as if she was considering leaving too.

Sheed would've known what to do here. He would've gotten angry and thrown something, or gotten excited and jumped on the table so every one could hear him, and they would've listened. Those were *his* maneuvers.

Otto turned to TimeStar. "Can you say something to them? You're an adult. They might listen."

Otto's grown-up self knelt and grabbed the boy by both shoulders. "I'm an adult, but I'm also you. Technically, this is your time, dude. You got this."

TimeStar released him, and he faced the room. "Hey, everybody . . ."

His voice was too low, drowned by clinking spoons and woeful moans. Otto took a deep breath and thought, *I got this.*

He shouted, "HEY, EVERYBODY! LISTEN UP!"

Every Clock Watcher in the place focused on him. Father Time stopped banging his head on the table. "Things have gone pretty wrong today," said Otto. "Some of that is my fault. Most of it is on Mr. Flux. I think you all know that."

Murmuring agreement rumbled throughout the place.

Otto said, "What's happening now, though, is *your* fault."

All that agreement mess stopped.

"What do you mean?" several Second Guessers said at once.

"Ice cream is delicious. I don't blame you for that. But this feels like Give Up Ice Cream, not Get Ready to Fight Ice Cream."

The Second Guessers grumbled some more; Otto thought they might jump him.

Father Time spoke up. "What would you have us do? Our function is managing time, and that's not important anymore."

"Your function has to be different now. You have to adjust. To save time. That's very important."

A disgruntled Minute Man with poor aim flung a maraschino cherry in the general direction of Otto's head. "Easy for you to say. You *human persons* are always flip-flopping about. Changing this plan. Changing that plan. All that flexibility is simple for you."

A lone Clock Watcher stood in the corner. He wore a vest that displayed a bunch of digital clock faces. They all kept flickering, changing, springing forward an hour, then falling back. He raised his hand and said, "I'm fine with flexibility."

The cranky Minute Man threw a handful of chopped walnuts at him. "Nobody asked you, Daylight Savings Time!"

Otto clenched his fists. "I usually have a partner, someone who helps me handle stuff. He's gone, and . . . I don't know if I'm going to ever get him back."

TimeStar, visible from the corner of Otto's eye, nodded. *Keep going.*

"I'm going to have to figure out how to do stuff on my own. I don't know if I'm going to be good at it. It might go super bad when we get out there and face Mr. Flux, but

I'm going anyway. If at least some of you help me, then we have a chance. Or just keep eating ice cream forever. It's up to you." Otto snatched a cherry from A.M.'s big bowl and tossed it at that Minute Man, dinging him right in the nose. "That's for Sheed! Now, who's with me?"

A.M. and P.M. put down their spoons. A.M. clutched her skirt and hopped off her stool. "We always liked the look of you," she said.

"Your determination is so chic," said P.M., joining her.

Game Time leapt onto Father Time's table. "Yeaaa-ahhhhh!"

The Second Guessers huddled together, conferred, then broke with a simultaneous clap. "We guess we'll help."

One by one, the remaining Clock Watchers joined in. Reluctantly, perhaps, but Otto couldn't afford to turn anyone away because of low enthusiasm. If that had been enough to disqualify participants, he'd have left Petey behind.

TimeStar slapped a hand on Otto's back. "I told you you had this. I'm really proud of us. So, what's the maneuver?"

"It's a new one. Maneuver #73: unstick our army."

34
An Easy Assumption

MISSUS NEDRAW, THE PROPRIETOR OF the Rorrim Mirror Emporium, had been the answer, proof that all was not lost. A.M. and P.M. had touched her, along with Otto and Sheed, and she'd been permanently unfrozen, free to chase her mirror monsters.

ENTRY #78

A Clock Watcher touch + a human touch = an unfrozen person.

DEDUCTION: Enough unfrozen Fry residents could rival Mr. Flux's Clock Watcher army.

Three unstuck humans—Otto, TimeStar, and Petey

—and not very many Clock Watchers meant they better get moving.

"We won't be able to unfreeze everyone, but I've got a few names in mind. A.M. and P.M., you're fast, can you two help zip me and TimeStar around the county?"

The Golden Hours nodded fervently.

"What about me?" Petey asked.

"I've got a different job for you. I just need to get you a lab partner." Otto explained what he meant, and when he finished, Petey grinned big.

TimeStar said, "Where do you want me to go first?"

"For now, we're sticking together."

"Why? We'll cover more ground if we split up." He stopped, considered. "I'm really debating with myself."

Another Grandma saying came to mind: *you boys could start an argument with your own reflections.*

Otto scribbled in his notebook, thinking as he wrote. "We'll split up soon enough. Gonna need your help with something big first."

"If you say so."

Otto ran around the ice cream shop, his notepad pages fluttering. Between the day's observations, deductions, and next steps, this maneuver was the most complicated yet. Very likely one-use-only. There'd be no second chances.

With everyone assigned their role, Otto asked, "Any questions?"

Father Time raised his hand. "If we win, can we have more ice cream?"

Otto said, "I'll see what I can do."

Petey explained to the Golden Hours that when they carried Otto and TimeStar around the county, they couldn't move at light speed. "Going that fast will disintegrate a human."

A.M. and P.M. nodded thoughtfully. "Good to know."

The Golden Hours going nowhere near their top speed were still pretty darn fast, getting Otto and TimeStar from the ice cream shop to the edge of the Gnarled Forest, where Wiki and Leen Ellison remained frozen.

TimeStar said, "Oh, wow! The Epic Ellisons."

"Me and P.M. will unfreeze Leen. You and A.M. get Wiki."

TimeStar moved toward Leen before Otto finished talking. "You take Wiki."

"Um, okay. I guess it doesn't matter."

TimeStar and A.M. worked on unfreezing Leen. Otto approached Wiki, and was not looking forward to it. "Listen, I'm going to unstick you now. I have to touch you to do it. Is it okay if I grab your arm?"

Grandma said they should always ask permission before touching people. No matter the circumstance, even if time was frozen.

"Yes, you can touch my arm."

Otto reached for her and motioned for P.M. to do the same. "I'm going to have to explain something kind of unbelievable to you."

Wiki said, "That old guy and you are the same person. He must be from the future. Which means time travel is a thing."

Otto snatched his hand back, semi-furious. "*How* do you know that?"

"I saw you two standing side by side. Even with him being older, you share thirty-two identical facial characteristics. Me and Leen don't have that many similarities, and we're twins. It's either time travel or some kind of cloning experiment. I estimated time travel was seventy-seven percent more likely. An easy assumption."

Huffing but forcing himself to focus, Otto grasped her arm. P.M. touched her shoulder, and Wiki sagged from her previous frozen state. Smiling, she flexed, bounced in place, shadowboxed the air with several quick jabs. A few yards away, Leen Ellison stretched, enjoying freedom, the gear in her tool belt clanking with each movement. "You okay, Wiki?"

"Good to go, sis." Wiki leaned into Otto and whispered, "Where's Sheed?"

"We're going to get him. We need your help."

Wiki dismissed that with a hand wave. "Of course you

need our help to get *your* Sheed, nothing new there." She jutted her chin toward TimeStar. "Where's *his* Sheed? The way you two are, how's grown-up you not with grown-up him?"

He didn't bother turning away or try to control his facial expressions. He didn't care to hide what he knew of Sheed's fate. It was a hard secret to have.

"Oh." Wiki sounded uncharacteristically . . . kind and sad. "I'm . . . I'm sorry." She touched his arm, and a tiny electric shock passed between them. Even though she hadn't asked first, it was okay.

"Don't be sorry yet. *Our* Sheed is in the clock tower, and he needs us."

"Then he's got us." She stepped closer, still touching his arm, and whispered, "Don't tell Leen about Old Sheed. You know how she gets."

Otto actually didn't know how Leen got, beyond her knack for building strange, dangerous machines. He nodded anyway.

Wiki yelled to her sister, "Hey, Leen! Time to go to work."

Leen's lip quivered; her head whipped between Wiki and the woods. "But my robot."

"Leave it for now. We'll come back—"

Otto stopped her. "Actually, I wasn't planning on leaving it."

According to his notes, big objects could be unfrozen when two people touched them—just like the upside-down levitating car on Main Street.

Otto delved into the shadows toward the massive machine. "Hey, TimeStar, do you mind giving me a hand?"

There were other stops to make, other allies to recruit. Mr. Archie and Anna, once unstuck, provided supplies from their hardware store. Dr. Medina wanted in on the fight, and promised her healthiest animals would help, too. (Otto didn't know how that was going to work exactly, but he wasn't in a position to turn away volunteers.)

Missus Nedraw, however, was not so willing.

"No," she shrieked, coiling a bandage around a circular, sucker-shaped bruise on her calf—an injury sustained wrestling the mirror tentacles. "I almost lost a prisoner because of your carelessness. I will not leave my post here at the emporium, and you cannot have any of the things you asked for. You created this problem, you fix it on your own! Do you hear?"

Otto had been afraid this might happen, so he gave P.M. the signal they'd discussed, and quickly (though not so quick that they'd disintegrate the warden) Missus Nedraw got zipped from the Mirror Emporium and dropped off fifty miles away at a Walmart in Richmond.

P.M. returned to Otto directing Clock Watchers and

county residents to gather the necessary items. When he was sure the plan was being executed to his satisfaction, Otto said, "Get me back to the lab while the others finish up here."

In a blink, he was at Petey's. P.M. gave a polite nod, then zipped away again.

Leen hunched over TimeStar's malfunctioning time travel device, Petey at her shoulder. The two of them grinned, heads bobbing in agreement. Otto hoped that was a good sign.

"What did you find out?"

Leen spun her chair so they faced each other, pointed at some new complicated drawing on Petey's corkboard. All graph lines, and swooping curves, and mathematical equations that looked like a language from another planet.

She said, "This device is fine as far as I can tell. There's no damage to it. All interior connections and circuits — if that's what you even call parts this advanced — haven't been disturbed."

"So why can't TimeStar go home?"

Petey said, "It was so obvious once Leen suggested it. Thank you, Leen."

"You're welcome, Mr. Petey." Leen bowed to the applause in her head.

"TimeStar's trying to go *forward* in time. There is no

forward when time is frozen. Unless we win, we're at the end."

Otto whipped out his notepad jotting that down, another deduction—and maybe one more maneuver—came to mind. "Okay. We're almost ready. Even if we weren't, we can't wait. There's no telling what kind of horrible things Mr. Flux is doing to Sheed, if he hasn't outright frozen him already. We have to rescue him now!"

Petey and Leen—especially Leen—agreed, wholeheartedly. The horrors Sheed was surely enduring were beyond imagining.

35
The Horror

"OW!" SHEED SCREAMED, pinching his wrist where Mr. Flux's minion had pricked him with her terrifying needle.

"Hold still, sir," said the Clock Watcher, making another torturous attempt.

Sheed tore his arm from the monster's grasp and pleaded with Mr. Flux. "Please stop. We don't have to do this."

Mr. Flux, his head cocked, evaluated the Clock Watcher's nasty work. "I think we do, Rasheed. That sleeve is a bit long. Don't you think so, Stitch?"

A Stitch in Time stood tall, snaking the yellow measuring tape over her shoulder and jabbing the offending needle into the pumpkin-shaped pincushion affixed to her wrist. "I refuse to deal with a human who can't appreciate quality tailoring." Frustrated, she huffed away.

Sheed stared at himself in Stitch's tall mirror and barely recognized what he saw. As Mr. Flux's new second in command, he was required to wear a suit, like when Grandma dragged them to church on Sundays. Sheed hated suits.

Particularly this one, a replica of Mr. Flux's black pants, black jacket, white shirt. The only thing missing was —

"Here's your hat." Mr. Flux shoved a familiar looking stovepipe hat at him.

When he'd agreed to the deal he'd been offered (really, what kind of offer was it — join or freeze), Sheed hadn't known about the dress code. If he had, he might've chosen freezing. His jeans, sneakers, T-shirt, and Flamingos jersey lay in a messy pile nearby. Abandoned so Sheed could become a mini Mr. Flux.

If Otto saw him now . . .

"Do I detect sadness, Rasheed? Are you reminiscing about your old life?"

"No."

"Because if you were, I'd remind you of how under-appreciated you were there. And how perfectly appreciated you are here. I gave you a suit. What do you say?"

"Thanks."

Mr. Flux placed the hat atop Sheed's head, the brim resting on his brow. "Now I have bad news. Your fantastic new suit is going to get dirty. You can blame your cousin for it."

"Otto? What?"

"Our people have been watching him run around the county, stirring up things. He's planning an attack soon. When he arrives, I want to be sure you're not confused about your loyalty." His hands caressed the camera around his neck; his thumb hovered by the shutter button. "Are you confused, Rasheed?"

Sheed plucked at the fabric of his new shirt, forced himself not to look at his jersey in the corner. "No. I'm not."

"Good." There was a mighty racket outside, crunching steel and shattering glass. Inside the clock tower, the legions of Clock Watchers scrambled, panicked. "Because your sweet cousin Octavius is here."

36
The Battle of Fry

OTTO MARCHED INTO TOWN SQUARE with his friends, his heartbeat thumping throughout his entire body. TimeStar was at his side, as was Petey. Anna Archie and her dad backed him up, along with Petey's mom (because Missus Thunkle wasn't letting her Lovebug go fight a Time War without her). Father Time and Game Time and the Second Guessers and the Minute Men and Dr. Medina, with a pack of assorted animals who all seemed to, oddly, follow her every command, were present. Mr. James brought his smoker and grill to the edge of the square. His thinking: "Y'all gonna be hungry after all that fighting."

If they were still capable of eating.

A single shot from Mr. Flux's camera could freeze them all, so Otto made sure to approach the clock tower from an angle where they couldn't be seen from some high window, easy targets. The closer they got, the more Otto understood that Mr. Flux had no intention of fighting at a distance. His Clock Watchers—dozens upon dozens—spilled from the tower, filling the square, meeting them head-on.

Then there were the Time Suck beasts. While the friendly one they'd left grazing by the Eternal Creek now roamed with Otto and friends, at least ten more were under the command of Flux's army, their duck bills raised high and their frightening honks echoing all through Fry.

The last and biggest Time Suck clambered down from the clock tower with Mr. Flux himself stuck on its back like a tick. He was not alone.

Sheed rode with him. Though he didn't look much like Sheed, dressed in a black suit and hat that matched Mr. Flux's.

Otto had feared his cousin was being tortured or was time frozen. This was worse.

Confident—really, just smug—Mr. Flux rode his Time Suck to the frontline, facing off with Otto. Only a thirty-yard gap and a statue of Fry's founder, Fullerton French Fryer, separated them. Raising his hand, Mr. Flux silenced the rowdy rumbling from his troops, who had to outnumber Otto's army three to one.

Mr. Flux halted his Time Suck, then stood tall on its back, like when Sheed stood on his bike seat while it was still rolling, nearly giving Grandma a heart attack. He surveyed Otto's troops, basked in his supremacy. "Welcome, everyone. I'm so glad you're here. It gives me such great pleasure to accept your surrender in person."

TimeStar gave a go-ahead nod. Otto cleared his throat, and said, "We want you to unfreeze time. Then leave. You're not welcome in Logan County."

"But I like it here. I've made new friends. Isn't that right, Rasheed?"

Sheed rose to his feet, much more wobbly than when he did the bike seat trick, but managed to find his balance next to his new twin, Mr. Flux. Both of their hats slanted in the same eerie manner as Sheed said, "Yep."

Leen Ellison did not take it well. "Sheed? What you think you're doing? You're going to fall and break your neck. Get down here! You belong with us."

"No, dear. He belongs with the winners." Mr. Flux raised the camera, aimed it at Otto's entire crew. "I'm going to give the smart ones among you the time it takes to run from your side to mine before I press this little button and turn you all into monuments like Fullerton French Fryer here. How's that—"

Sheed tapped Mr. Flux's shoulder.

"Yes, Rasheed."

Sheed swung a swift roundhouse kick into Mr. Flux's groin.

Flux "ooofed!" clenched his knees together, then toppled sideways on his furry steed's broad back, accidentally firing off a camera shot that froze a Time Suck and several members of the Flux army to his immediate left.

Flux's Time Suck was startled by the flash; it shuffled side to side, knocking down nearby Clock Watchers. Still, Sheed remained on its back with the stunned Mr. Flux and shouted, "Dude, that's my cousin down there. I'm always picking him over whoever. No matter how big a jerk he is."

"Thanks, Sheed," Otto shouted back. "I think."

Cheers erupted from Otto's army. Otto yelled to Sheed, "Get the camera!" To everyone else, "Charge!"

Sheed bent over Mr. Flux, snatching at the camera strap. The kick didn't keep Flux down long. His arm stretched, and he grasped the Time Suck's tail, yanking himself away from Sheed's grasp while aiming the camera at him.

"Oh no you don't." TimeStar hurled a mousetrap provided by Archie's Hardware Store. It cartwheeled end over end, snapping onto Mr. Flux's shooting hand. He yelped, firing another inadvertent camera flash, catching a few of Otto's Second Guessers. The short and stout Clock Watchers shouted, "Crud!" in frozen unison.

Sheed abandoned the camera-grab mission and dived off the Time Suck's back. He grabbed a thick tuft of fur on the way down, breaking his fall while also causing the beast to honk and buck in pain. Mr. Flux hung on for all his worth.

"Sorry," Sheed apologized to the beast. He released the

fur, hit the ground in a roll, popped to his feet, and sprinted through the chaotic battle. "Otto!"

"Sheed!" Otto rushed into the thick of it. Ducking, dodging, hopping over all the little skirmishes that broke out.

Game Time and Crunch Time engaged in a particularly sweaty and determined fencing match, their improvised swords—a fireplace poker and a snow shovel handle—whizzing and clanking. Dr. Medina's entire menagerie of animals—dogs, cats, snakes, a wild-eyed goat, even a quartet of guinea pigs—launched coordinated attacks at her prompting. The veterinarian barked, and the dogs fell on a squadron of Business Hours, chewing through their briefcases and shiny leather shoes. Switching to meows, she directed the cats in a stealthy flanking attack. The goat battered a Clock Watcher that made a swiping grab at Otto. The guinea pigs used Otto's head as a springboard, flinging themselves at a large Time Suck's eye.

Sheed caught glimpses of his cousin through the melee and did what he could to assist other combatants as he attempted to reunite with Otto. Some well-timed tripping and shoving helped sway a couple of small fights. The battle raged in every direction, though.

As part of a two-pronged attack, P.M. flashed around various assailants at high speed, leaving mirrors confiscated from Missus Nedraw's stuck in midair. Having been instructed by Otto, the closest human executed the second part of the attack by unfreezing a mirror so it shattered on the ground, unleashing the groping monster prisoner inside, which attacked Flux's troops without mercy.

Leen Ellison made her way to the top of the founder's statue, where she flung what looked like small Frisbees from her tool belt. The discs sprouted thin, wiry legs like spiders and skittered into the crowd, where they affixed themselves to Mr. Flux's troops, delivering electrical charges that sent them yelping up and out of the fray.

Anna and Mr. Archie got in the act, swinging a rake and a length of plastic pipe respectively, swatting Clock Watchers like giant bugs.

And Father Time! Oh, Father Time . . . danced through the battle with a wooden cane he twirled like a ninja's staff. He jabbed and parried and thrust, cutting a path any way he wished.

At every position, anywhere on the Fry Town Square battlefield, the brigade Otto had assembled fought valiantly.

It wasn't enough.

Mr. Flux had the numbers. The camera. No longer stunned by Sheed's betrayal, enraged, screaming, he aimed the lens into the crowd and fired. Lightning-bright flashes doused swaths of combatants, freezing them mid-punch, mid-kick, mid-retreat. It didn't matter if they were his troops, or Otto's. His wrath had no targets, just release.

Sheed kept pushing his way to Otto, seeing the residual camera flashes from the corner of his eye like quiet lightning in a distant cloud.

Leen spotted him from her statue perch, took a moment to cutesy wave at him, then cupped a hand to her mouth. "Wiki! A.M.! Now!"

In a blur, Wiki Ellison appeared next to her sister, dropped off by the speedster Golden Hour, who'd already zoomed away. Sheed stopped at the statue base and watched the sisters bicker as usual.

Leen said, "Where is it? You didn't hurt it, did you?"

"It's been chasing me all over town," Wiki snapped. "It's coming. Have a little faith."

Sheed yelled up, "Hey, what's the plan?"

Wiki said, "Get to Otto. We're good here."

More flashes popped, more fighters on both sides were frozen and out of the fight. If they didn't do something about Flux soon . . .

"Go!" Wiki insisted. "He needs you!"

Sheed left the girls, kept pushing through the crowd. The ground vibrated in mini earthquakes. What was happening?

Otto leapt over a mirror tentacle and one of Dr. Medina's

snakes as they slinked toward a terrified Flux fighter, and wrapped his arms around a startled Sheed.

"You're okay," Otto said, soaking Sheed's suit coat with sloppy tears.

Sheed hugged back. "Why are you crying? I thought legends didn't do that."

"I'm amending our rules."

The ground shook more powerfully, knocking the boys off balance.

Sheed said, "I don't know if we're okay yet. What is that?"

"Maneuver #74."

Sheed shook his head. "A new maneuver?"

Otto grinned. "Yep. 'Bring in the robot.'"

Over his shoulder Sheed spotted the chrome dome and glowing red eyes of Leen's robot lumbering into the fight. Its head rotated as it locked on to a waving Wiki and Leen at the founder's statue. "Over here," they shouted.

Mr. Flux's flashes were rapid-fire by then, with photos of frozen fighters spooling from the camera and falling to his feet like large, square confetti. So preoccupied with his power, he didn't notice Wiki leaping from the statue, weaving through the remaining fighters, and positioning herself so the robot was on a direct course for her, with Mr. Flux between her and the metal giant.

"Hey, Flux Face," Wiki yelled.

That snatched his attention. He aimed the camera at her.

Wiki pointed over his shoulder. "You got bigger problems, buddy!"

A long shadow fell over Mr. Flux. He turned to find the robot looming over him, too close to freeze.

Leen pointed at Mr. Flux, yelled, "Robot! He's 'it' now. Tag him."

Mr. Flux said, "Oh. Oh no!"

One bolt-studded metal hand smacked Mr. Flux, sending him airborne in an odd blur of cartwheeling motion. He landed in a pile about twenty feet away from the boys, the camera knocked from his grip.

Dazed, he tried to push himself to his feet, reaching for the camera. The robot's rusty metal palm fell on him like a swatter falling on a fly. Cracks webbed from the asphalt beneath Mr. Flux. The robot's hand rose, fell again. And again. Tag-tag-tag!

Mr. Flux squawked, "Ow, ow, ow," with each slap, as he flattened into a Flux pancake.

The camera remained on the ground near his hand, though, as no one seemed willing to get close while the robot delivered its awesome smackdown.

The girls sprinted to Otto and Sheed. Wiki said, "Is that enough?"

A golden blur of light, almost too fast to see, rushed between Otto and the camera. Otto said, "Now it is."

Wiki gave her sister a nod, and Leen yelled, "Robot! We're 'it' again, me and Wiki."

Its red eyes leveled on them.

"We're going to lead it away. It's your show now," Wiki told Otto on the run. She shouted over her shoulder, "Don't mess it up."

Leen said, "Bye, Sheed."

The Epic Ellison Girls exited the battle, their rogue robot in pursuit, their part of the maneuver complete.

The rest is on us, Otto thought. "Come on. Time to fix the day." He whistled, calling over the friendly Time Suck. Though not fast enough.

The recovering Mr. Flux's limbs and torso retracted quickly from his smooshed, flapjack form to something resembling a human. He whipped his stretchy arm toward his lost camera, reclaiming it. "Octavius and Rasheed, I think you two need a break."

He aimed, fired.

The flash blinded the world.

37
Exit, Stage Left

TIMESTAR LEAPT BETWEEN MR. FLUX and the boys at the last possible second, taking the full brunt of the flash.

Now immobilized, he spoke through barely parted lips, "You better make this worth it. Go, guys."

So they did.

Using already-frozen combatants as cover, the boys rushed to their Time Suck and shimmied up its side. Otto gently coaxed the beast into motion, while Sheed yelled at Mr. Flux, "If you want us, come get us."

Whipping his bendy limbs about, Mr. Flux mounted the nearest Time Suck, digging his heels into its flank, forcing it into a run while he attempted another shot. The camera flashed but missed as Otto and Sheed's Time Suck made a sharp right and darted from Town Square.

Mr. Flux's Time Suck bucked after them like a marshal

chasing stagecoach robbers in the old black-and-white Westerns Grandma liked. From Town Square to Main Street, from Main Street past the park, past the park toward that steep hill leading to Fry High. Otto and Sheed hugged tightly to their Time Suck's fur as it dipped and dodged Mr. Flux's repeated attempts to freeze them in their tracks.

Bounding up the hill to Fry High, the creature barreled through the hole it created earlier, following its original course to the library. Otto tugged lightly on the fur he gripped, turning it in a different direction. "Not this time, girl." He guessed it was a girl.

In the quiet halls, Mr. Flux's angry shouting carried. "Is this another desperate ploy for some way to defeat me? More yearbooks? So futile."

Otto and Sheed's Time Suck galloped full speed toward a set of double doors.

"Hang on!" Sheed said, pressing his face into soft fur.

Otto ducked his head an instant before impact.

The Time Suck tore through the wall, destroying the doors and the sign above it in the process. Despite the jarring impact, Otto and Sheed were fine. They climbed from the beast, weaved through time-frozen debris, then sprinted to the front of the room.

Sheed craned his neck, taking in the vast space. "What now? Hide?"

"No." Otto kept them in the open, onstage, the center of attention. As was this room's intended purpose.

"But he's—"

Coming. Mr. Flux—not to be outdone—forced his beast through a different section of wall, creating more destruction. He didn't seem to notice where he'd been driving his Time Suck until this very moment. Otto had counted on this.

The sign over the door, the one they destroyed with their crashing entrance, had said AUDITORIUM.

"Come on," Otto said, climbing up onto the stage.

"He can see us."

"I know."

Sheed's natural inclination to fight his cousin buzzed

stronger than ever. Yet he followed because that's what they did. That was all there was to it. Through arguments, through temptation to rule beside Mr. Flux. So if they got frozen for all of time on that stage, at least they'd be together.

Mr. Flux halted his Time Suck, took in his surroundings. "Oh, I see."

He leapt from the beast's back, strolled coolly down the aisle between the many rows of seats meant for student assemblies and choir concerts. And plays.

Mr. Flux's smile was genuine. "You're trying to appeal to some sort of nostalgia, aren't you? I was created in this room. Perhaps you can convince me that I should do things differently. That I can be a better person."

He made a flying leap, landing on the stage mere yards from Otto and Sheed. "You boys are sweet, courageous champions of your county. The lazy, undriven residents don't deserve you. Which is perfect, because they won't have you much longer."

He raised the camera, aimed. "It's a shame we couldn't work together. You two will make lovely monuments to my triumph, though. Are you ready?"

Sheed cut his eyes to Otto, waiting for some signal. Another maneuver.

Otto only said, "Whenever you are."

"Such brave boys." Mr. Flux pressed the shutter button, and a sun-bright flash obliterated shadows for a microsecond.

Then all was still.

Otto and Sheed remained as statues. Mr. Flux drew closer, admiring his latest trophies. "I know you can hear me, and I understand if you don't want to respond, though I am curious. What did you really hope to accomplish here? All you did was prolong my inevitable victory."

"*Inevitable* is a very strong word. Don't you think, Sheed?"

"Sure do, Otto."

The boys moved.

Effortlessly.

Unfrozen.

Panicked, Mr. Flux leapt backwards. He aimed the camera, fired another flash. The boys winced at the bright light, but approached Mr. Flux slowly, still unfrozen.

"How?" Mr. Flux examined the camera, then fired again. And again. And again.

Sheed had the same question, but knew his cousin well enough to get that they'd all have answers soon enough.

Otto shouted, "Come in, everyone."

Two blurs zipped into the auditorium. A.M. and P.M., carrying TimeStar and Petey. The Golden Hours placed the two men on their feet, and they climbed onto the stage beside Otto and Sheed. Petey handed a familiar device to Otto.

The real camera.

A bug-eyed Mr. Flux examined his own device, perplexed.

Otto explained. "Wiki and Leen's robot was the key. It was big enough to distract you, and strong enough to knock you around while my fast friends swapped cameras. They've been hanging on to the real one"—Otto held it high—"ever since."

"You think you're so smart, don't you? Well—" Mr. Flux lunged away, attempting to exit stage left.

Otto's nimble fingers handled the camera with ease, aiming and snapping a photo. The flash left Mr. Flux stuck in his sprinter's pose, arms at runner's angles, one knee high. The accompanying photo spilled from the camera into Sheed's waiting hand.

Otto said, "All the shots you took after the switch produced no pictures. It's the one thing Petey couldn't get the replica camera to do. Thank goodness you were too mad to notice. We were counting on that."

"Why?" Mr. Flux spat from unmoving lips. "So you could convince me to unfreeze your world and let all of you unmotivated humans continue wasting time and opportunities? Well, you're going to be disappointed. I don't care that I'm frozen, it's not so different from all the years I spent stuck watching you people squander all your time! I know what happens if this freeze isn't undone. If I stay stuck, Fry stays stuck. I still win."

Now, that was alarming. Mr. Flux had a point, and Sheed didn't know what to do about it. He flicked his eyes to Otto, whose face was pinched with concern, but not *dire* concern. More like *tricky maneuver* concern.

"What now?" Sheed said.

TimeStar held his time travel device in his palm, triggered it with his thumb. A pair of blue lasers shot from the device, tracing a tall, wide rectangle — a door — in thin air.

"Maneuver #75," Otto said. "We're going back in time."

38
Maneuver #75

WITH THE BLAZING BLUE DOOR open, Otto asked Petey, "Are you ready?"

Frowning, Petey nodded. "As I'll ever be."

Otto motioned to A.M. and P.M. The Golden Hours grabbed frozen Mr. Flux.

"Get your hands off me!" Mr. Flux protested.

A.M. said, "This is a really good look for you, darling."

"Trust us," said P.M. "We're experts."

They pushed him through the time door.

Petey clenched his fist and ran through before he could chicken out.

TimeStar said, "You two first."

Otto linked arms with Sheed. Sheed said, "This seems risky."

There was hesitance in Otto. Most people wouldn't have noticed, but Sheed had been around him too long. When

Otto craned his neck and locked eyes with TimeStar, there was something weird there. Something scary. *What?* Sheed didn't know.

Otto faced Sheed. "It's only risky when we don't have each other's back. Come on."

Together, they leapt into the light.

There was a whooshing sensation. Sheed's stomach dropped, like they were in an elevator going down too fast. When the sensation became so powerful that Sheed thought he might be sick, it stopped and they were on the stage again. Did it not work?

"Hey!" some strange new voice shouted. "What are you doing on my stage? You're interrupting my rehearsal."

They weren't alone in a time-frozen auditorium like they'd been a moment ago. No, all around them Sheed saw motion. Flowing dresses and veils. Boys primping in badly fitted suits like his own. A young Donny O'Doyle as Abraham Lincoln, his glued-on beard peeling at the sideburns, while he clutched a young Petey Thunkle by his paint-stained overalls. There was a slip of paper in Donny's hand — the letter inviting young Petey to the Turing Unified Research and Development Institute. The letter that started all their problems.

Old Petey Thunkle, who had spent the last decade downing himself, doubting himself, discouraging himself, disapproving himself, and finding some way, every day, to consider himself disqualified from any good that might come from his smarts, did not see the letter as the problem. He'd made that clear to Otto before they set out on this adventure. Otto had come up with the plan to make this right. Maneuver #75 was Petey's and Petey's alone.

Everyone else was backup.

"What is this?" said frozen Mr. Flux, unable to intervene.

"This is you not winning," Otto whispered near his ear. Then, loudly, "Go for it, Petey."

Old Petey approached Young Petey, who still struggled in Donny O'Doyle's tight grip. At that moment, a young, camera toting Anna Archie entered the auditorium, wearing a perplexed expression. Both Old Petey and Young Petey became fixed on her. TimeStar intervened, assisting the Peteys by tapping Donny on the shoulder. "Come on, let him go."

Not bold enough to challenge an adult, Donny released Young Petey. TimeStar plucked the Turing letter from his hand, passed it to Old Petey, then guided Donny away. At an appropriate point, TimeStar planted a boot in Donny's coattails and sent the boy flying off the stage. A short yelp and hard thud later, he was sprawled in the floor, his castmates rushing forward to coddle him, leaving Old Petey and Young Petey alone to talk.

Anna continued down the auditorium aisle. "Petey, are you okay?"

Old Petey passed Young Petey the letter. And Young Petey told Anna, "I think so." Then, to his older self, "Thanks, sir."

Sheed leaned into Otto, speaking hushed and fast. "That should be it, right? Donny doesn't call it TURD Institute. No Mr. Flux."

"Not exactly." Otto recognized Sheed knew some version of this story, likely from Mr. Flux himself. But, when crafting this plan, Petey told Otto the rest. Why changing this moment was important, but not enough.

Old Petey went about his mission. "You may not believe me right now," he told his young self, "though I think you will the more you consider it. I'm you. From the future."

Young Petey stepped backwards, checking the best escape routes for getting away from the crazy people quick, fast, and in a hurry.

"Don't get that look in your eye; my friends and I aren't here to hurt you. If you're afraid of me, then I've already completed half of what I came to do. You should be plenty scared of becoming this." He jabbed his index finger into his own chest.

It sounded like Petey's usual downer talk, though it wasn't. He was a desperate man, trying to save his own life and the lives of everyone in Fry the only way he knew how, by convincing himself not to give up on . . . himself.

"I work in Mr. Archie's hardware store," said Old Petey.

At that Anna stiffened and looked ready to object, but Young Petey gave a slight nod and mouthed, *We're fine.*

Old Petey said, "It's honest work, and I'd be proud to be someone like Mr. Archie. I'm not even that. Today starts a pattern in your—*our*—life where we shy away from anything that seems hard, or scary, or maybe we'll fail at. Donny was going to tease us and make fun of everything that letter in your hand says. That's on him. When we believe him and let his idiotic words stop us from chasing our dreams, that's on us. There will always be Donnys, people who want to tell us no, and can't, and shouldn't. I've known that for some time but have yet to do anything about it. Now I am. I'm begging you to not become me. Don't take ten years to figure this out. Don't let it be Otto, and Sheed, and TimeStar, and Wiki, and Leen, and the Clock Watchers who help you see what you can be. Do you believe me?"

Young Petey's eyes brimmed. "Yes. You have the same scar on your eyebrow that I have from—"

"The propeller of the hovercraft we built when we were six. Will you go to the Turing Institute? Will you promise? Will you promise to keep trying after that? No matter the negative stuff you hear, especially if that negative stuff is coming from you?"

A crying Young Petey nodded.

A single slow clap pattered offstage; the drama club director, overwhelmed with feels, applauded. As did his lead actress and the boy playing John Wilkes Booth and, louder than all of them, Anna Archie. Petey, both versions, got the first standing ovation of their life.

Including Mr. Flux. Unfrozen, somehow.

He clapped along, shed tears. Otto, Sheed, and Time-Star leapt into defensive positions in case he attacked.

Otto aimed the camera at him, attempting to freeze him again. The shutter button wouldn't budge. He shot a panicked look at Sheed, who yelled, "Maneuver—"

"That won't be necessary." Mr. Flux held up a halting hand, a hand that seemed less substantial suddenly. Less there. The time-freezing, Clock-Watcher-dominating, cruel and calculating villain of the day was fading like smoke.

His hand became see-through; his black suit lightened to gray; from the stage you could see rows and rows of burgundy velvet seats right through him. If you were in those seats, you could see the play's set and backdrop through an increasingly translucent man shape.

Part of Otto found this horrifying. How Flux was all there a moment ago, and slowly, surely, wasn't. When he pulled his eyes away from Mr. Flux to Sheed, he didn't feel better, all too aware that the fate TimeStar described for his cousin wasn't so different.

Sheed did not see the horrors Otto witnessed. He saw resolve. Mr. Flux, whom he'd spent a little time with, wasn't being snatched painfully from the world. It seemed easy; he accepted it. Maybe that was why he smiled.

The Peteys seemed to recognize some grand new beginning in the disappearance of Mr. Flux. A whole new world of possibilities. So only Otto freaked out when Old Petey began to fade, along with the troublemaking camera in his hands.

All the trouble Old Petey's missed opportunity had caused was being erased from existence.

Otto let the disappearing camera fall, now so light and insubstantial, it arced back and forth slowly, like an autumn leaf released from a tree branch, before it touched the stage lightly. The device was not his primary concern. "Petey, no! Not you."

"It's okay," Old Petey said, his disappearance speeding up. "This is what we came here for."

Otto's head whipped to an almost completely faded Mr. Flux, who grinned and agreed. "I never *wanted* to be the bad guy, Octavius."

In an instant, the camera, Old Petey, and Mr. Flux vanished.

The auditorium doors crashed open as Principal Prince —who was still Fry High's principal in modern times— burst in with one of Young Petey's fellow stagehands, who'd apparently run for help when Otto, Sheed, and friends appeared from nowhere.

"That's our cue," TimeStar said, adjusting his time device for forward motion. That it now worked, allowing travel into the future, was a good sign.

Sheed asked the obvious question, though. "How do we know what we're going back to?"

TimeStar and Otto spoke at once, in an eerie harmony that raised goose flesh on Sheed's arms. "Only one way to find out."

The blazing time door yawned opened. The three of them jumped through, into the unknown.

They did not look back.

39
UFO

OTTO WAS FIRST, THEN SHEED, then TimeStar, the brilliant blue portal snapping shut behind him. Stepping onto the stage of the empty auditorium, it was hard to tell if they'd come back to the right day, year, or century.

"Where are A.M. and P.M.?" asked Sheed.

There were no telltale golden footprints anywhere.

TimeStar shrugged, rechecking the digital display on his device. "Says we're in the right time."

The auditorium doors were intact—no stampeding Time Suck damage. The three of them pushed through into the empty outer corridor. Then outside of the school —which was also not damaged. The entire building looked whole and unscathed.

The day remained hot and incredibly still. Descending the Fry High hill, Otto's stomach flip-flopped. Had they failed?

A familiar, old-timey red car—last seen upside down near Mr. Archie's store—motored by. Its driver, the car collector Mr. Green, gave a short horn blurt and a wave.

Otto, Sheed, and TimeStar followed the car's path to the intersection; it stopped while other unfrozen cars passed, then turned into traffic.

The three of them erupted into cheers. They hopped up and down, high-fived, danced. Time was as they'd always known it to be before Mr. Flux came to town.

Or so they thought.

Main Street was alive with Fry citizens bustling on about their day. All the lampposts stood upright. All the cars sat on their tires. No debris was frozen in midair. Sheed and Otto were ecstatic about another successful adventure.

TimeStar said, "When Petey stopped his younger self from creating Mr. Flux, it must have sent a ripple through time so none of the terrible things we left behind ever happened."

Otto leapt onto the curb when some little kids kicked scooters past him. "Grandma's not frozen, then?"

"She shouldn't be. No one should be."

"What about Petey?" Sheed said. "Why'd he disappear like that? Where did he go?"

Otto pointed up the street. "Let's go where we usually find him."

The door chimes at Archie's Hardware signaled their entrance, and they were greeted by a young, pimply-faced clerk they'd only ever seen in a yearbook photo. His orange apron said SYLVESTER. He asked, "Can I help you?"

Careful, Otto said, "Mr. Archie around?"

"Oh, yeah. He's shelving some glue guns in the back."

They moved into the depths of the store and found Mr. Archie doing just as Sylvester said, shelving new, shiny aluminum glue guns next to carpet shampooers.

Sheed said, "Yo, Mr. Archie?"

He turned, and he wasn't the jolly, rosy-cheeked man who always greeted them with a smile. Same face, same height, a bit more bulge to his belly. Not cheery, though, not the guy who loved elephants. Something was wrong here. "Otto and Sheed. What can I help you with?"

"Uh . . ." Otto couldn't find his words. The change in the man was so apparent and disturbing.

"Well," said Sheed, shaken by this new, sadder Mr. Archie.

TimeStar stepped in and shook Mr. Archie's hand vigorously. "How you do, Mr. Archie? I'm Otto and Sheed's older cousin, and I was telling them I used to be friendly with some kids who went to Fry High back in the day. Guy named Petey was one of them, and the boys said they thought he worked here sometimes."

Mr. Archie's face crinkled. "Peter Thunkle? Work here?

Otto and Sheed, you know better than that. I wouldn't trust that thief with a single nail in this store. Not after what he done." He snatched a dusty handkerchief from his back pocket and dabbed at his eyes. "Excuse me, I got a shipment of plungers I need to unpack."

Disappearing into the back room, his diminishing sniffles trailing, Mr. Archie left them among the empty guns. Glueless and clueless.

"A thief?" said Otto.

Maybe the new Petey wasn't the improvement they'd hoped for.

After a quick call home to check on Grandma ("I'm fine boys! Why wouldn't I be?"), they spent the last day of summer wandering around town. Sheed was still in his black suit, though the stovepipe hat had gotten lost somewhere in time. No one questioned this new, formal look of his. Everyone in Fry had seen stranger things.

They got some barbecue from Mr. James, petted some puppies at Dr. Medina's. Tossed a Frisbee with some Fry High kids until they were tired and gasping. TimeStar let them lead, Otto noticing how he'd sneak glances at Sheed any and every chance he got.

Without a word, and no outward sign of agreement, they stuck to safe, normal, unlegendary activities. After the Mr. Archie surprise, they feared what else may have changed due to their time meddling, so they seized onto every rec-ognizable thing they could, lest they be surprised by some other drastic unexplained shift in some once-familiar per-son's looks, speech, or anything, really.

All that wandering wore them out something terrible, though. With no bikes, they began the long walk back to Grandma's.

The street they strolled had sparse, country-lazy traf-fic that never exceeded the speed limit. Every passing car startled starlings into flight. The clouds meandered, the sun slid across the sky. A dog barked somewhere far away.

Their bright yellow house in the middle of green wavy grass appeared on the horizon like a sunrise. TimeStar said, "I should probably return to Harkness Hill. See about get-ting back to my own time. Wouldn't be good if Grandma saw me."

Sheed cocked his head. TimeStar's mention of Grandma had been a little too casual.

"*Your* grandma," TimeStar said. "*Yours.* She'd probably think my clothes were weird."

Sheed squinted, scrutinized TimeStar's face. Otto leapt between the two of them. "That's probably a good idea. We'll walk with you. You lead the way."

The whole march up Harkness, Otto made a point of positioning himself between Sheed and TimeStar, hop-ing to prevent what would be catastrophic recognition. For surely if Sheed recognized a grown-up Otto, he'd also recognize his adult self's suspicious absence.

Guarding Sheed from the truth presented a different problem for Otto. He wanted one last, private, desperate word with TimeStar. Something he couldn't do with Sheed on his heels. Sadly, he could think of no maneuver to change the situation.

On top of Harkness, where they'd first met Mr. Flux, TimeStar peered over the county with longing. "It doesn't look like this in my time."

Otto would've asked how Logan County had changed, despite warnings of knowing too much about the future. But, a whiny, chopping sound unlike anything he'd ever heard snatched his attention.

Sheed shielded his eyes from the sun as a triangular silhouette unlike anything he'd ever seen hovered closer.

TimeStar took a protective stance. "Get behind me boys."

They did as told—Otto feeling extra strange being protected by himself—and watched a sleek, metallic vehicle descend quickly over the grass before them, then hovering just feet from the ground before making a gentle touchdown.

It was something like a helicopter, painted a metallic gray-black like the photos of a stealth bomber in Otto's airplane encyclopedia. Angular nose, wide middle that narrowed into an aerodynamic tail. It had no visible propeller, though blue light similar to TimeStar's device gleamed beneath it. The dark tinted windshield prevented a view of the pilots. Stenciled on the side was a stylish logo, a red circle around yellow letters: PT.

A side door jutted forward, breaking some kind of seal with a pressurized hiss, then slid aside giving them a view of plush leather seats occupied by two almost familiar people.

Popping his chrome safety harness, a barely recognizable Petey Thunkle leapt nimbly from the cabin. "Hi there, fellas! Long time no see."

40
The Last Deduction of Summer

THE SAME WAY THAT MR. ARCHIE was unexpectedly down, Petey, in his tailored gray suit, fancy haircut, and eyeglasses that looked cooler than eyeglasses should, was unexpectedly up! He was perky, and bright, and excited.

Was that what messing with time did? Made people you know switch personalities?

Sheed, happy to see Petey and happier to see such a weirdly neat vehicle, couldn't keep away. He flung himself at Petey, and Otto followed suit, nearly tackling the changed man.

Through the rough and welcome hugs, Petey snaked a hand free for a shake from TimeStar, who asked, "What happened to you?"

Petey glanced over his shoulder. There was another passenger in the vehicle, their face hidden by shadow. He leaned forward, whispering, "I listened to me. Old me.

Went to the Turing Institute. Then MIT. Then built some prototype engines that would go on to revolutionize daily travel leading to the Interstate Skyway System, then —"

Sheed formed a T with his hands. "Time-out. What's a skyway?"

Petey laughed. "It hasn't expanded this far out yet, but by the time you two take flyer's ed and get flyer's licenses, there should be several hover lanes operational in this part of the country."

Otto felt lightheaded. "Are you saying you invented flying cars?"

"Not exactly. The engine. Not the car. Well, they're not really cars. Lev-Ports is the technical name. No need to split hairs."

Sheed gasped, possibly hyperventilating. "YOU INVENTED FLYING CARS!"

The passenger in Petey's . . . Lev-Port, spoke up. "Darling, are you okay out there?"

There was something about that voice.

Petey waved with his left hand, a silver band on his left ring finger, like TimeStar's. "I'm fine, dumpling. Chatting with friends." To Sheed, "Yes. If we're keeping it simple, flying cars are a product of my company Petey-Tech. Though that's nothing compared to my greatest invention."

He motioned to the time travel device dangling from

TimeStar's belt. "Haven't quite figured it out yet, but I'm close. Obviously, I succeed. Or none of us would be here."

"About that," Otto said, referring to his notes. "How are we here like this? You disappeared, and the world changed. Why do we remember Mr. Flux and the Clock Watchers?"

Petey shrugged. "I could get into a lot of dense theories on space and time. Could explain that since we were all disjointed from the time freeze for such a long period, the time-changing ripple effect hit us differently than everyone else. Or I could give you the best, though not particularly scientific explanation. Logan County makes everything weird."

Otto chewed his pencil. How to document that?

ENTRY #80
Logan = Weird (always).

Sheed traced a finger over the PeteyTech logo. "Why'd Mr. Archie tell us you're a thief? He used to love you like a son."

Petey gave a mighty eye roll. "He still loves me like a son. He has to. He's cranky because, well . . . Anna, could you come here a sec, honey?"

Anna Archie (or was it Thunkle now?) stepped from the Lev-Port in a shimmering gown, with large diamonds strung like ice cubes on her necklace, the stones winking sunlight. Though none of them compared to the boulder weighing down her left hand.

"Hi, everyone." She didn't seem to recognize Otto and Sheed. That stung, but Logan = Weird (always). She looked healthy and happy. Her smile hadn't changed a bit.

Petey's fingers intertwined with hers. "Your dad is still saying I stole you out of Fry."

Anna shook her head. "No one can steal me. I go where I want. And I wanted to go with you. I knew you were destined for big things." She punched Petey's shoulder, playful. "When we're done here, let's take Dad for a ride in the Lev-Port. He loves seeing the other side of the clouds, so he'll forgive you for one night."

Petey said, "Duty calls, fellas."

"Wait." Sheed pointed to the Lev-Port cabin, "Can I see inside?"

Otto's heart sped up. *Please say yes, Petey.*

"Sure." Petey said, "You too, Otto?"

"No thank you. I'm all teched out."

Sheed frowned. "Suit yourself."

He leapt into the vehicle, leaving Petey admiring the landscape with Anna, and TimeStar looking at Otto warily. "You want to talk."

Otto said, "Come on."

Leading TimeStar, Otto circled the Lev-Port as if admiring the exterior, in case Sheed could see them from inside. That vehicle was the farthest thing from Otto's mind. He flipped his pad open with one hand, referred to his notes. "I've figured it out, you know."

"Figured what out? I don't know what you're talking about." There was lightness to TimeStar's words, the sound of playing dumb. Otto expected as much.

"You lied about a bunch of stuff. I think you had to because there are real rules to time travel, and you were skating dangerously close to breaking them. The things you're not supposed to change. *Things*. You said it over and over again for a reason."

"Yes," TimeStar confirmed.

Near the Lev-Port's tail, away from prying eyes, Otto faced the traveler. "And you lied about coming back to see us battle the Laughing Locusts."

"Why on earth would you make such an accusation?" A grin was starting to form.

"Because your device takes you to the same location in the past or future. It's why we had to lure Mr. Flux to the auditorium, so we could be *in the auditorium* the day Petey created him. That means in the future, you opened your portal on Harkness Hill to drop in on Mr. Flux. You meant to be on the hill. Today."

TimeStar rocked back and forth on his heels, crossed his arms, puckered his lips as if he might start whistling casually. Faking innocence.

Otto flipped through his pages quickly, checking notes and deductions from the day. He continued. "When we were on the roof with Witching Hour, you said the time freeze gave you wiggle room with the rules of time travel. You chose today so you could do something you wouldn't be allowed to do on a day when time was functioning normally."

TimeStar twiddled his thumbs, having fun now. "Time travel is heavily regulated in the year I'm from. So much so that when anyone attempts it, our Time Bureau can easily track them to almost any day and place and snatch them right back."

Almost any day. "They can't track you here. Because of all that happened."

"Here and now confuses their equipment. You can't ever say Logan County strangeness isn't good for something."

"Why all the lies? The superhero nickname, the fake year, made-up stories about sightseeing trips through time?"

"You know. Be honest."

That was the tough part, wasn't it? "I wouldn't have believed you if you told me the truth."

TimeStar said, "You—*we*—need to deduce things on our own. We don't trust information that comes too easily. Even on a day when time froze, I didn't have time to try and convince you why I was here when I knew you'd figure it out on your own. And was I right? Did you?"

Otto did. "When Leen Ellison confirmed your device

still had the ability to travel backwards in time, you didn't object when I suggested Petey go back and talk to his younger self to fix his life, even though you'd said over and over that you're not supposed to change things about the past."

TimeStar's grin faded, his gaze seemed to pierce Otto. "So, what's that final deduction?"

Otto flipped to a specific page, the one he'd written on back at Mr. Archie's store, when he and Sheed found the upside-down car. He reread it, asked himself if he was absolutely sure. He was. "You can't change *things* about the past," Otto reiterated, then showed TimeStar his answer.

ENTRY #39

DEDUCTION: People aren't things.

Otto said, "Old Petey gave Young Petey just a little information, and *Young Petey* changed. Look what happened. Flying cars!"

"And?"

"You *want* me to change. To be better, less selfish, less jealous." Otto could hear Sheed squealing over whatever cool thing he'd found inside the Lev-Port. "So I can save him."

TimeStar clapped slowly. "Deducing has always been my favorite."

"How? You said the sickness is in his blood. That he can't be saved."

"Under normal circumstances, that's absolutely true." He spread his arms wide, as if to hug all of Logan County. "But look where we are. I mean—and this is just a wild thought—what if you weren't so concerned with picking adventures that would get you more Keys to the City?"

Otto pondered that. "You're saying I should focus less on adventures that would make us more legendary, and more on stuff that might help Sheed?"

"I didn't say that. You did. Though I guess that's kind of the same thing, right?" He winked and unclipped the time travel device from his belt, made adjustments. "I think it's time I got back now."

"Wait! Grandma says that bending rules isn't that different from breaking them if the rules matter. Are you going to get in trouble with the Time Bureau when you get home?"

TimeStar shrugged. "Some trouble's worth it."

Triggering the device, a portal opened, an electric blue rectangle.

Otto said, "You're not going to say bye to Sheed?"

Deadly serious, TimeStar said, "If you do your job, I'll never have to."

Otto nodded, accepting the mission.

TimeStar stepped halfway through the portal, then stepped out again. "You know, if I'm already in trouble, I might as well give you a freebie."

Otto fought a chill, braced for potentially horrifying revelation. "What?"

"Wiki Ellison," TimeStar said, "ain't so bad."

"Wiki?"

A crackling arc of electric blue lightning snapped from the doorway to the silver ring on TimeStar's hand. The wedding ring.

"Wait. You don't mean—"

"Good luck, Otto. It was great seeing you again." TimeStar jumped fully through the door, it winked shut behind him, leaving Otto with the same unbroken view he'd started the day with.

It was so much stranger now.

41
Maneuver #3

THE BREEZE RUSTLED THE GRASS across the fields between the boys and Grandma's house. In the sky, Petey's Lev-Port became a smudge over it all, growing smaller and smaller, until it vanished in a cloud, leaving Otto and Sheed alone for the first time in what felt like a long while. The longest last day of summer ever.

"At least Petey said 'peace out.'" Sheed scrunched his face. "That TimeStar jerk just has no manners."

"He did a lot for us today," Otto said. "Could you try to go easy on him?"

"Why do you care? You know something was off about him. He had shifty eyes."

Otto nearly protested—his eyes were not shifty—but decided to let it go. There were more important matters. Instead, he said, "You're still wearing Mr. Flux's suit. Grandma's going to have questions."

"Unless you distract her and let me sneak in."

"Maneuver #3? Sure, that could work."

"Not yet, though."

Sheed sat on the hill, a great westward view of the sun sinking over distant trees. The golden light—the best of the day—reminded Otto of something. Digging through his pocket, past his notepad, he touched a slim, stiff piece of paper. Pulling it free, he read the newest souvenir—a business card they'd be adding to their bedroom shelves.

GOLDEN HOUR, A.M.
"Your Best Look Now"

Sheed said, "What do you think happened to the Clock Watchers?"

"I guess they went back where they belonged. Time's moving again, so they're probably busy. Especially now." The sunlight at this hour cast everything in streaking bronze, making it all picture worthy. Otto wished for a camera, then immediately regretted it. He'd rely on his memory, at least for a while.

Staring down the hill at the dancing grass beneath them, there was a flickering shimmer in the air. For just the slightest moment, Otto thought, perhaps, he saw the hazy, yellow-clad outlines of his friends, A.M. and P.M., waving at him. The light shifted, however, and there was nothing there. Sadness hit, then hit him again when he turned to Sheed to ask if he'd seen them, too.

I'm going to save you, Sheed, Otto thought. Though not today.

Today they'd enjoy summer as it was meant to be. A temporary thing made richer by its inevitable end. Tomorrow, a new adventure. And the next day. And the next.

"Why are you looking at me like that?" Sheed said. "Like goofy?"

Otto lied. "I was thinking about how many Keys to the City we need to shoot for so the Ellisons never catch up."

"You really have an ego problem. Good thing I'm here to keep you in check."

"I agree. Let's go see what Grandma's cooking. After I sneak you in."

"Cool. If it's pie, you can have my slice."

"Really?"

Sheed reconsidered. "Part of my slice."

They talked pie, and new adventures, and the Ellisons all the way home with the love of cousins.

Best friends.

Really, brothers.

A legendary bond that wouldn't be broken. No matter what came their way.

This season, or beyond.

Appendix: Maneuvers

Maneuver #1 — Run

Maneuver #3 — Distract Grandma

Maneuver #14 — Breaking and Entering (Don't Tell Grandma)

Maneuver #16 — Corner and Capture

Maneuver #19 — Hi-Low-Sit

Maneuver #21 — Stand Your Ground

Maneuver #22 — Duck and Cover

Maneuver #24 — Guarding Flanks

Maneuver #38 — Rope Wrangling

~~Maneuver #42 — Jumping the Creek~~

Maneuver #73 — Unstick Our Army

Maneuver #74 — Bring in the Robot

Maneuver #75 — Time Travel

Acknowledgments

This is new territory for me. Not writing acknowledgments—I've certainly done that before—but the kind of off-kilter, kooky fun (and tears) of the pages leading here represent a different sandbox than what I'm used to playing in. It was a joy to write Otto and Sheed, though the joy wasn't all mine. A lot of people helped, and they deserve some shine.

First, Adrienne, whom the Interwebz knows as "Dear Wife"—you're always fun, funny, sympathetic, and patient when it comes to this crazy "book stuff." May we have many more road trips filled with off-key singing and laughter. Love you!

Mom, I love you too. Those back-in-the-day library trips and book purchases that probably stretched our available time and money helped make this possible. I will never be able to thank you enough, though I will keep trying.

Shout-out to the rest of my family. That's siblings, in-laws, cousins (especially the cousins), aunts, uncles, and so on. There's not enough space to name you all here, though I will call out two in particular: Aaliyah and Jaiden, my niece and nephew. You were on my mind a lot while I documented the happenings of Logan County and the town of Fry. I hope you have as much fun there as I did.

Kwame Alexander, I'll never forget that text from 2016 that set all this in motion. Thanks for always being a great friend and offering such generous advice and opportunities. #TeamVersify.

Speaking of Versify, thanks to Margaret Raymo for guiding me through the care and maintenance of this manuscript while entertaining my ramblings about time travel, alternate dimensions, DuckTales, and PowerPoint presentations. Erika Turner, thanks for your sharp eyes and insightful questions. Lisa DiSarro, thank you for helping get this book in front of the people who want and need it. Whitney Leader-Picone, thank you for your direction on the super cool design of this book. And Dapo Adeola, man, your art is simply magical. I can't express how exciting it was every time you took words from the page and turned them into beautiful people and creatures.

Jamie Weiss Chilton and the rest of the Andrea Brown Literary Agency, thanks for constantly guiding me through so many of the intangibles that lead to our joint successes. Eric Reid and William Morris Endeavor, thank you for seeing the potential in my work and opening up new avenues for all of us. Carmen Oliver of The Booking Biz, thank you for making sure I get to go out and shake the hands of the many readers, librarians, teachers, administrators, and conference organizers who support the work I do.

Meg Medina and Jason Reynolds, thanks so much for reading early drafts of this thing and giving me pointers on how to better approach this world. Everyone knows what incredible writers you both are, and I'm happy to report that you're also incredible friends.

Last but not least, thanks to the crew I've established along the way . . . there are SOOOO many of you: Ellen Oh, Aisha Saeed, Marieke Nijkamp, I. W. Gregorio, Miranda Paul, Olugbemisola Rhuday-Perkovich, Dhonielle Clayton, Sona Charaipotra, Tiffany Jackson, Daria Peoples-Riley, Nic Stone, Angie Thomas, Tracey Baptiste, Jeff Zentner, Eric Smith, Gretchen McNeil, Jennifer Wolfe, Preeti Chhibber, Juanita Giles, Alison Green Myers . . . and . . . AND . . . SIGH . . .

And if I'm leaving anyone out, it's the head, not the heart. Thank you all for all you do. Now on to the next adventure.

Read on for a preview of the next
Legendary Alston Boys adventure!

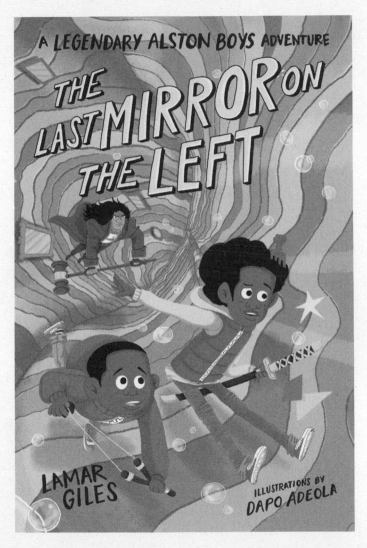

kangaroo court

(noun) a court held by a group of people in order to
find someone guilty of a crime or misdemeanor
without good evidence

1

Sheed's Probably Going to Punch Otto

IN THE OPINION OF SHEED ALSTON—one half of the duo known as the Legendary Alston Boys of Logan County—his cousin Otto (the other, more annoying half) sometimes needed to be punched.

Sheed had come to the conclusion a few years ago, when Otto got on this whole dinosaur thing. Don't get it twisted—dinosaurs were, and still are, super cool! But even something super cool, like dinosaurs, became less cool when Otto insisted on knowing every single fact in the world about them, then insisted Sheed know that he knew every single fact in the world about them. All day. Every day.

Like, okay, Otto, a lot of movies got it wrong, because some dinosaurs had feathers . . . but did he ever think movies don't show that because then the dinosaurs would look like chickens and that's just dumb?

Around the fourth time Otto mentioned that the

heaviest dinosaur was the Argentinosaurus and it weighed ninety tons, Sheed had had enough. He'd slugged Otto in the chest.

Not a hard punch. He didn't want to *hurt* Otto. It was just enough to make a point. Otto stopped talking about dinosaurs so much after that.

And now that Otto was onto a new topic, one so much less cool than dinosaurs, Sheed knew another punch was coming. For sure.

"Did you know," Otto said, "doctors who play video games are twenty-seven percent faster than doctors who don't?"

It was Saturday in Logan County, Virginia. The sun was shining. The leaves were shifting from green to brown/orange/gold, and they hadn't had any legend-worthy cases lately so Sheed wanted to eat his Frosty Loops with just the right amount of milk—the loops only damp, not soggy—in peace. Then maybe ride bikes to Fry Park and do flips off the swings. He did not want to talk about doctors. Again.

"Faster at what?" Grandma sang. She had choir rehearsal that afternoon, and while she worked the dough for the biscuits she was taking to the church, she also practiced. Low notes, high notes. Their conversation was at least one half song. Sheed didn't like this tune, though.

"Diagnosing illnesses," Otto said. "And surgeries. They make fewer mistakes, too. Do you think Dr. Bell plays video games?"

Grandma cut off a high C note and resorted to her speaking voice, giving her vocal cords a break. "I don't know about that. Dr. Bell likes fly fishing, I heard him speak on that many occasions."

"People can like fly fishing and video games, Grandma. Maybe you should make an appointment for me and Sheed, and we can ask him."

Sheed dropped his spoon into his Frosty Loops bowl, splashing milk on the table. He leaned into Otto and whispered through clenched teeth, "Are you crazy?"

Visiting Dr. Bell usually meant *shots*. That man was scarier than the dentist and were-bears combined.

"We're overdue for checkups," Otto said, looking at the floor. "They're important."

"Stop. Talking." Sheed flexed his punching hand.

Grandma left her biscuit dough alone and checked the teacup-pig calendar on the wall, humming while she flipped back a few months. "Y'all went at the beginning of summer. We barely into fall, so you don't need a checkup yet." She crossed the kitchen, rubbing dusty flour on her apron before pressing the back of her hand to Otto's forehead. "You feeling all right, sugar?"

Sheed wondered the same thing.

"I'm fine, Grandma." Otto still wouldn't meet Sheed's eyes.

"What about you?" Grandma said, reaching for Sheed. Sheed tried to execute Maneuver #1 (run), but Otto turned full traitor and grabbed his wrist so he couldn't get away. He was so getting punched when they were alone.

"Hold still," Grandma said sharply, and Sheed knew better than to resist.

When she pressed her hand to his forehead, she said, "Hmm."

Grandma then grazed his cheek. "You do seem a bit warm."

"I'm fine, Grandma. It's just hot in here from the oven." He slipped away, headed upstairs, cranky because he knew his Frosty Loops were too soggy now—the optimal milk absorption window was a narrow one—and he was almost certain his cousin had just bought him a trip to Dr. Bell's. What was wrong with Otto?

"Rasheed Alston! I know you ain't stomping up no stairs in my house!"

Sheed stopped stomping. "No, Grandma."

Otto padded out of the kitchen but skidded to a halt at the base of the stairs when Sheed gave him the *we have unfinished business* look they saw all the time in kung fu movies. Otto said, "Um? Where you going?"

This! On top of doctors-doctors all the time, Otto acted like he couldn't let Sheed out of his sight for one second these days.

"To brush my teeth!" Sheed said. At the top of the stairs, he entered the bathroom and slammed the door.

"Rasheed Alston! I know you ain't slamming no doors in my house!"

"No, Grandma."

He sat on the edge of the bathtub, cupping his chin in both hands. If there was a way to mess up a Saturday, leave it to Otto to discover it.

A couple of sharp knocks sounded. Sheed yelled at the door, "Leave me alone."

Two more knocks, like he hadn't said a word. Not from the door, and not even close to the sound you get when knuckles hit wood. This sound was a hollow echo. Maybe a pipe? The house was old so that happened sometimes. He leaned into the bathtub, ear angled toward the drain.

Two more knocks, followed by a voice that almost made Sheed run screaming.

It said, "I know you're there, Mr. Alston. I'd prefer not to be rude about this, but you and your cousin have already worn my patience razor thin."

Sheed stood slowly, tracing the sound to a place it should not be coming from: the mirror over the sink.

When he faced it, the usual sight — his own reflection — was not where it should be. Instead, the mirror had become something like a window, looking into an all-too-familiar building. The Rorrim Mirror Emporium in downtown Fry.

Obscuring the view of the massive mirror warehouse was the magically weird proprietor of the emporium.

"Missus Nedraw?" Sheed said.

"Of course it's me. I require you and the annoying one's assistance. Get him now. Chop-chop!"

Sheed had no idea what this was, but he and Missus Nedraw agreed on Otto being annoying, so that was something.

2
Upon Further Reflection

GRANDMA GOT BACK TO HER BISCUITS, and Otto returned to the kitchen table, sulking, to finish his Frosty Loops. He wasn't hungry anyway. His appetite had taken a real beating in the last few weeks.

It was Saturday in Logan County, Virginia. Clouds kept blotting out the sun—and Otto usually liked clouds. The leaves were drooping and dying. It was starting to get chilly, which meant everybody at school would be sniffly with extra snot. Otto missed how things were before the last day of summer, when everything had gone so terribly wrong.

Since that day, there'd been so much on his mind, so many observations and not nearly enough deductions. All about his cousin. None more important—and terrifying—than the one that changed everything.

If Otto didn't do something, Sheed was going to die.

Maybe not next week, or even next year, but there was no timeline that Otto would accept. Hadn't he himself come from the future — as the traveler TimeStar — to keep from losing Sheed? Didn't he have to do everything in his power to complete the mission TimeStar had given him?

He shoved his Frosty Loops aside and left Grandma to her singing and baking. He drifted into the living room and flopped in his favorite spot on the old lumpy couch, where he fished his notepad from his pocket. Otto did his best thinking on paper.

OTTO'S LEGENDARY LOG, VOLUME 24

ENTRY #25

Sheed's not going to ever WANT to go to the doctor, and I can feel him getting super annoyed with me. It's the dinosaurs all over again. BUT, if it saves his life, I'll be annoying.

DEDUCTION: Keep working Grandma. If she believes Sheed is sick, she'll MAKE him go to the doctor, and we can maybe get a JUMP on whatever's wrong with him.

Of course, it had occurred to Otto that he might simply tell Grandma what he knew. Or tell Sheed. Every time he felt he might break and spill it all, he was reminded that he — *TimeStar*— hadn't conquered the laws of time and space, hadn't come back to Logan County from decades in the future, to run to Grandma. TimeStar also hadn't revealed his true identity to Sheed. It was a secret Otto was meant to keep. And fix. On his own.

To save Grandma the pain he'd felt when he deduced there was no future for Sheed. To save Sheed the knowledge of death chasing him with much less distance to make up than anyone would've expected. To—

"Otto! Come up here, please."

Uh-oh. Sheed said please. I'm definitely getting punched now, Otto thought.

But it would be worth it if Otto saved him.

"Why do you want me to come up there?" Otto wasn't necessarily eager to catch hands.

"I can't find the toothpaste. I need your help."

Nope. Not falling for that. "It's where it always is."

"The *special* toothpaste. Now, get up here!"

The special—? Oh, this was one of the new maneuvers. #83: Put *special* in front of something that's *not* special, so you know something actually special—*Logan County Special*—is happening.

Grandma was too busy kneading her dough and

humming her church songs to catch on, so Otto slipped away, stuffing his notepad into a pocket on his cargo pants while creeping upstairs very carefully, in case the Logan County Special thing had Sheed hostage or something.

At the top landing, Sheed's head protruded from the bathroom, his Afro pick wedged tight in his hair, and he waved Otto over. If this was a punching trick, it was a good one, because Sheed didn't look annoyed at all. He looked scared.

"What is it?" Otto asked.

Sheed grabbed his shirt, yanked him inside, then shut the door behind them. "Look."

He pointed at the mirror that wasn't doing what a mirror was supposed to. It looked more like a TV screen, and Otto did not like the footage being displayed.

Otto said, "Missus Nedraw?"

She cleared her throat. "Yes, I'm right here."

"Ack!" Otto shouted.

"Ack," Missus Nedraw said, drolly, "is correct. There's more 'ack' than I care for going on today, and you two are going to help me fix all the 'ack.'"

Otto said. "What's wrong?"

Missus Nedraw sneered. "Of course you have no clue. You think you can do whatever you want and your choices won't affect those around you. It's the same sort of short-sighted inconsiderate behavior that lands my prisoners where they are. You two should be glad we're addressing this early. With my intervention, perhaps I can turn you . . . you . . . *criminals* from your wayward path before it's too late."

The boys had only recently discovered the truth about the Rorrim Mirror Emporium. That it was a prison. The various mirrors it housed were cells, the prisoners locked behind the glass. Missus Nedraw was the warden.

Otto and Sheed accepted what should've been an over-whelming discovery because it was made on that strange last day of summer, and honestly, there were weirder things happening. Now the idea of a secret mirror prison hidden in downtown Fry, and the truly insulting comment Missus Nedraw just made, required some revisiting.

"Don't call us criminals!" Sheed said. "Grandma told us not to let anyone call us out of our names. We haven't done anything wrong."

"In fact"—Otto kept his voice low because he didn't want Grandma hearing, though he was about to make a good point that deserved to be heard—"we're the premier heroes of this county. The opposite of criminals. Legends. Thank you very much."

Missus Nedraw nodded sharply and paced on her side of her the mirror, with her arms clasped behind her back, giving them a full view of the crowded emporium floor as she left the mirror frame, then returned, blocking their view until she disappeared on the opposite side.

She didn't look like her normal, put-together self. Usually

she wore wool jackets over frilly blouses with high collars, long skirts, and striped socks with boots. Her mouth was always pinched, her glasses spot-free, and her silver-black hair pulled into a flawless tight bun. From what Otto could see of her, the outfit was about the same, just messier. The jacket seemed smudged with crusty stains. One lens of her glasses was cracked. Stray hairs protruded from her scalp at odd angles, like she'd had an unfortunate run-in with some aggressive static electricity.

Otto grabbed his notebook while she wasn't paying attention, scribbled furiously.

ENTRY #26

Missus Nedraw looks like a hot mess.

DEDUCTION: Something's happened at the emporium. Something bad.

She retraced her steps a few times, appeared to be thinking mightily. Then she stopped in the dead center of the bathroom mirror frame and said, "So you'd like the court to believe that you are not criminals?"

"We're not," Otto and Sheed said at once.

Then Otto thought, *What court?*

Missus Nedraw said, "Tell me, then, who took mirrors

from my emporium, without permission, to fight a being named Mr. Flux several weeks ago?"

The boys said nothing.

"Need I remind you," she said, "that you are under oath?"

Sheed said, "No, we're not. What?"

Sheed looked to Otto, perplexed. Otto shook his head. He didn't know what she was talking about either.

Missus Nedraw wobbled a bit, like she was dizzy, or weak. It didn't stop her crazy talk. "Well? Who took mirrors from the emporium?"

Reluctantly, Otto raised his hand.

"What's it called when you take something that does not belong to you, without permission?" she prodded.

Otto couldn't bring himself to say it. Mostly because he knew she wasn't wrong.

"Stealing," she finished. "You two stole from me. That is a crime."

Otto didn't like lies. Almost as much as he didn't like secrets. But he needed to clear up one thing. "Sheed didn't have anything to do with it."

Which was true, because Sheed had been Mr. Flux's captive when Otto orchestrated his plan.

Sheed, however, jumped in. "He did it to save all of Logan from being frozen forever. How do you even remember?"

That was a good question. They'd changed the past, and

to the best of Otto's knowledge, no one should remember the true events of the last day of summer outside of him, Sheed, TimeStar, and Petey Thunkle. Yet . . .

Missus Nedraw said, "The emporium and I are a part of the Multiverse Justice System. A constant throughout time and space, boys. Temporal reality may bend, but the law does not!"

Sheed said, "What the heck does that even mean?"

"It means your little stunt had consequences. Grave ones. That you need to help me rectify. We've wasted enough time. Come to me before I come to you. You have one hour."

Missus Nedraw slapped a palm flat against her side of the glass, and the mirror became a mirror again, displaying the boys' terrified faces.

Sheed said, "What does she want?"

"I don't know," Otto said, twisting the doorknob, "but she said one hour. I don't think we want to be late."

More from Versify for middle grade readers!

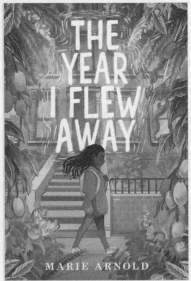